MORE PRAISE FOR *LOST BOI*

"Sassafras Lowrey takes us on a journey through queer time and space through the lens of the Peter Pan classic. Through rowdy imagery (which we don't even have to try hard to imagine), we get to journey with Pan, Mommy Wendi, and John Michael through the Neverland squat to learn (and unlearn) all the perils of growing up."
—**Cristy C. Road, author of** *Spit & Passion* **and** *Bad Habits*

"At the heart of Lowrey's loving, amazing, and crafty re-telling of the Peter Pan story is love and freedom, replete with bois and grrrls, sexy, sassy mermaids, leather pirates, and a melange of preferred gender pronouns, rollicking fun, and danger that will leave readers longing to never grow up, yet embracing becoming a new kind of grownup. Of the many adaptations of the classic Peter Pan tale, J.M. Barrie would rise up and cheer *Lost Boi*."
—**Charles Rice-Gonzalez, author of** *Chulito*

"I always suspected that something kinky and delicious was going on between Pan and his bois, but the leather and protocol role-play seen in Sassafras Lowrey's Neverland is only one part of queering this fairytale. Lowrey queers the entire monomyth narrative by shifting the perspective away from Wendi and allowing an insider—Tootles, lead boi in service of Pan—to tell the story. With an authentic and dire point of view, Tootles knows exactly what is at stake for his chosen family of tough lovers and lost bois."
—**Amber Dawn, author of** *Sub Rosa*

ARSENAL PULP PRESS ✚ *Vancouver*

a novel

Lost Boi

SASSAFRAS LOWREY

ARSENAL PULP PRESS
Suite 202–211 East Georgia St.
Vancouver, BC V6A 1Z6
Canada
arsenalpulp.com

Arsenal Pulp Press acknowledges the xʷməθkʷəy̓əm (Musqueam), Sḵwx̱wú7mesh (Squamish), and səl̓ilwətaɬ (Tsleil-Waututh) Nations, custodians of the traditional, ancestral, and unceded territories where our office is located. We pay respect to their histories, traditions, and continuous living cultures and commit to accountability, respectful relations, and friendship.

Cover photograph: Lyn Randle / Trevillion Images
Map illustration by Andrea Juby
Book design by Gerilee McBride
Editing by Susan Safyan

Printed and bound in Canada

Library and Archives Canada Cataloguing in Publication:
Lowrey, Sassafras, 1984–, author
Lost boi / Sassafras Lowrey.

Issued in print and electronic formats.
ISBN 978-1-55152-581-5 (pbk.).—ISBN 978-1-55152-582-2 (epub)

I. Title.

PS3612.O97L68 2015   813'.6   C2015-900401-2
                                             C2015-900402-0

For all the lost bois and grrrls.
May you grow up only if and when you are ready.
May we always remember the magic.

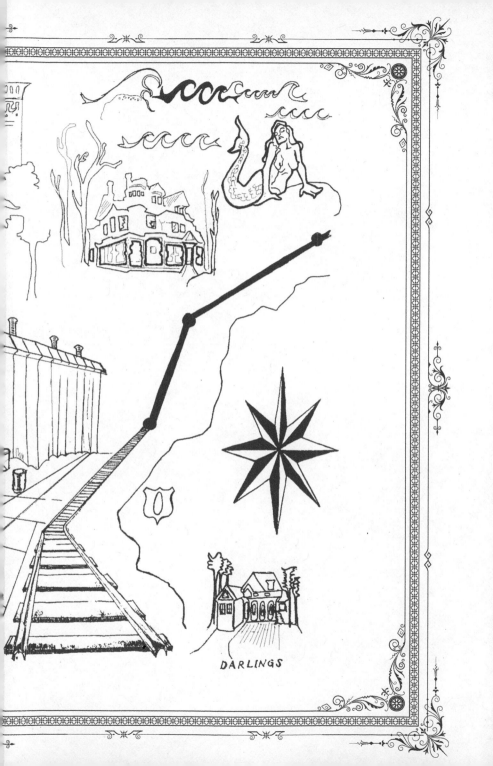

DARLINGS

Pan Breaks the Ice

*A*ll bois, except one, become grownups. They go to college or work in construction. They sign domestic partnership, civil union, or even marriage certificates. Some bois become artificially inseminated, have top surgery, or work in an office or as PE teachers. They go to law school or work in non-profits. Growing up happens to the best of us, even when we've said it wouldn't.

Wendi thought she wanted to be one of us. She said she wouldn't grow up and swore her allegiance, in blood, to Pan. Then she turned and grew up anyway. Guess I can't blame the grrrl; it's not like I've done any better.

Before Wendi, it was just Pan and us, his lost bois. Our life was a gritty Disneyland. We made the magic and the rules. No one told us when to go to bed, who to fuck, or where we could or couldn't pierce ourselves. Us bois all had our own pasts we were running away from, but none of that mattered anymore because we were Pan's. He was our Sir, and we swore ourselves unquestioningly to him. Every day was a new adventure. I loved Pan more than I've ever loved anyone. It was a different love than for a boifriend or grrrl-friend; it was deeper, more complete. I didn't just love Pan and our Neverland home; my life was consumed by a passion for something much bigger than any of us—this life we built with him, a world without grownups.

When Pan found her, Wendi lived in the Darlings' halfway home. She never knew her parents, having fallen out of her pram and gotten lost or something, ending up in foster care as a baby. When she started high school, Wendi was placed with the Darlings. Before that, she'd had a series of truly unfortunate placements, but she never talked about them to any of us. Pan cracked his knuckles and told us that she'd escaped from the worst kinds of grownups, who had no business being around children, especially grrrls. Wendi said the Darlings were okay as far as grownups were concerned. That wasn't saying much, if you ask me.

The Darlings' home was as loving as it could be, under the circumstance of it also being a business. Mr Darling spent hours late at night downstairs at the kitchen table, counting cheques for each of the kids in his care. He subtracted groceries and shoes, doctors' appointments and school supplies from the meager cheques the government sent to compensate them for the children they took into their home. There was never as much left over as he wanted there to be, and he would ask Mrs Darling to cut costs wherever she could. It

was a complicated arrangement; they wanted to do right by these disadvantaged children, but it was a lot of work, and Mr Darling believed that he and his wife deserved to be justly reimbursed for their civic good deed.

Since her arrival at the Darlings' house at 14 London Street, Wendi had shared a room with John Michael. It was crowded but comfortable, and unlike other places she'd been placed, the Darlings were less concerned about what she was doing, as long as the cheques kept coming. Wendi always considered herself lucky that, unlike John Michael, she could hide her difference behind her long hair and skirts. John Michael never grew out of her tomboy tendencies and was called a dyke and a lezzie in the locker room as she changed out of her softball uniform into baggy jeans and T-shirts. Everyone at school knew John Michael was queer, especially after she had Wendi cut off her hair in the little bathroom across the hall from their room. Everyone at school also thought Wendi and John Michael were dating because they sat together in the cafeteria and were the only out lesbians at school. Wendi never thought of John Michael that way. She revelled in being like a big sister and having a family of her own for the first time. Besides, even if she had been interested, she would never let herself go to that place, knowing that it could ruin everything, that she could be sent away and someone else could be cashing her cheque. In other houses, Wendi'd had to listen to lectures about morality and even get dragged to church services. She'd known enough to stay quiet about her queerness before, and when she talked of that time, she would always remark that she'd been grateful that the Darlings never seemed to pay attention. Still, she knew better than to push her luck, and she certainly didn't want to ruin things for John Michael, who'd had it worse than her: this was the first time she'd been placed with a family at all. Before the Darlings, it was all big group homes, punctuated by hospitals and juvie.

Wendi was a good student, and by the winter of her senior year, the fat college-acceptance envelopes began to arrive for her. Mr Darling would leave them on her bed. He was proud of the girl. Not many of their wards had such ambitious plans for the future. It pleased him to think that Wendi wouldn't continue to be a burden on taxpayers. He always tried to get the children who passed through his house to understand that they had been quite costly to society and that they needed to make amends as quickly as possible. At night, when Wendi got home from GSA meetings or rehearsals for school plays, she would sit quietly on the corner of the little single bed chewing the ends of her hair, and carefully open the envelopes. There was no question in her mind that, come next September, she would be out of the Darlings' home forever and strolling across manicured lawns in the shadow of ivy-covered buildings. She'd been waiting for that day her whole life, for the day when she would be surrounded by learning, when she would be an adult capable of making her own decisions and having them respected. Wendi dreamed of growing up, which makes it all the more surprising that she fell so hard for Pan.

When Wendi wasn't studying, she was writing. At first, it was mostly poetry. Pan said that Wendi was the best writer he'd ever heard; that's what first drew him to her. Wendi had always written little stories, and some other students in the GSA introduced her to the weekly open mic at a feminist bookstore downtown. It was not too far from Neverland, though she didn't know that yet. Wendi became a regular, reading stories each week about dykely prince charmings who swept beautiful femmes away to happily-ever-afters. At these events, Pan always stayed near the door at the back of the room. He'd never had much interest in lesbian open mics, so it surprised all us lost bois when he started going, alone, each week to the bookstore. He said there was something about Wendi's stories that he just couldn't resist. When he got home to Neverland, he'd crawl up into my hammock and tell me about this grrrl who told stories about kids like us, the way that she made us shine and sparkle so that everyone understood us. He talked about her pretty brown hair, the way it spilled over her shoulders, and the way her chest heaved and her eyes sometimes filled with tears when she read. Wendi was all feeling. Pan said he knew that what she wrote about was real because the words flew from her glossy pink lips, unsteady yet strong. Us bois were experts at finding the magic and making the hard shit sparkle, but we weren't so good at feeling. Pan was real cocky; he could get any boi or grrrl he wanted—and he still can. But something was different with Wendi.

I kept saying that he should go up to her after she read. "Sir, you are the bravest and most handsome boi. She wouldn't say no to you," I'd tell him again and again. Pan never did get the nerve to approach Wendi; his dog Erebos did it for him.

Erebos was a little pit-bull cross with a deep-bluish-black coat and a white star on her chest. Pan pulled her out of the dumpster where her litter had been thrown by an evil grownup. All the puppies died except for Erebos, whom Pan bottle-fed with a washed-out syringe and some puppy formula he shoplifted from the pet shop by the river. Grownups will cross the street when they see us coming with Erebos, but she only looks mean, like us. Grownups are always making assumptions, thinking they know everything about a dog or a boi before giving any of us a chance. Pan named the dog Erebos after the Greek god of shadows, and she never once left his side, except for when she went after Wendi that night. Pan had been watching Wendi read when Erebos jumped onto the stage, pulled at Wendi's backpack, and ran off into the crowd. Wendi had been reading a story about a femme princess kneeling before her buxom prince, hands bound behind her back, but she raced off the stage after the strange shadow of a dog. Pan, laughing, ran after her, and together they chased Erebos through the bookstore as she wove in and out of queers sitting on folding chairs then out onto the sidewalk. Pan tried to tackle Erebos, missed, and crashed into a phone booth. It was then that Erebos came right up to Wendi and dropped the backpack with a wag of her tail. Pan, who had picked himself up off the pavement, was forced to introduce himself. Wendi had, of course, noticed him sitting in the back of the room all those weeks, but she didn't let on.

It was the next morning that Mrs Darling first learned about Pan. She knew, of course, where the children kept their diaries and made a regular practice of reading them. Like all parents, she liked to know what was happening in her children's minds. If she could have, Mrs Darling would have tidied things up, ripped out pages, and burned them in the fire, but she knew the real world was not so simple. Still, she was concerned when she read in Wendi's diary about someone whose gender she could not determine who seemed much older, and yet, as Wendi described in excruciating detail the baggy sweatshirt, work pants, boots, and red hair, this...this person seemed perhaps to be no older than the children in her care. Mrs Darling was worried that this mysterious—boy? woman?—who lurked at the back of the room at open mics could be just the kind of distraction that her Wendi didn't need.

The Stars

I'm sure by now you are wondering who I am and what business I have telling these stories that aren't mine. Well, at least not entirely mine. The name's Tootles. I was lead boi in service of Pan, leader of us lost bois in Neverland. Who are the lost bois, you ask? To be a lost boi, you must be brave, strong, and above all loyal, but beyond that, we're hard to define. To write about who we were and what we always had been feels inadequate. Never in my life has there been anything as important as pleasing Pan. Magic is the only word for it. In Neverland I felt like anything was possible. Pan was a strict leader, but he brought bois alive and gave us a world few others ever saw.

It wasn't always easy. Sometimes it seemed like I missed all the big adventures. I'd be out dumpster diving so we could have dinner, and when I got back, there'd be blood every-where. I never minded, really, nor would I have hesitated to pull my knife and fight for Sir if I'd been called to. Sure, our world was violent, it had to be, but it was also bonfires, fucking, and skinny-dipping in the river. Often I was the only boi who Pan would talk to. I loved that. Until Wendi came, he'd always tell me about the mischief he'd gotten himself into, like fighting with the urban primitives outside the food co-op or tricking the pirates into thinking their house had rats. Fun shit like that. Sometimes Pan would go after bigger things, like pilfering a boi's Child-Protective-Service records from the briefcase of a new social worker, or starting things up again with Hook—but now I'm getting ahead of myself.

Above all else, Pan believed in the power of make-believe. I never knew which stories of his to really believe, but I also knew better than to doubt. When you became Pan's, you swore an oath that you would never doubt or question him. That's what kept the magic alive. Truth is a funny thing: it matters the most to grownups. To us bois, it never was very important. Besides, Pan has always liked a good story, especially if it's about him. I just liked Pan; he was everything to me back then, and I would've done anything if I thought it pleased him, but no matter how special our bond, I never could compete with Wendi. A grrrl is worth more than twenty bois, he would remind me when my jealousy got the better of me. I didn't understand what was so special about grrrls, especially that grrrl. No, actually, Wendi was a good Mommy to us all, and I served her with nearly as much loyalty as I showed Pan. It's just hard to talk about him and the way we were back then, after everything that's happened, but again I've said too much, and you don't even know the story yet. The last thing I want is to disrespect him more than I already have.

I was telling you about myself, though there isn't much to say. I fell out of my pram, and no one came looking. Little bois who don't get claimed (and we're never claimed because no one ever wants us) are sent away to all kinds of places. I was one of the lucky ones. I made it to Neverland.

I'll never forget my first night with him. Pan found me at the all-night diner, sitting alone in a booth, drawing. My pack was propped up on a chair like a silent dinner guest, and I was curled into the booth, trying not to fall asleep in my fries. I sipped coffee, which I hated because it made me think of my dad. The bells on the door jingled as Pan walked in, black boots beaded with rainwater. He sat at the counter and ordered a chocolate milkshake, pulling off his green baseball cap, running those little tattooed hands through his fiery red hair. I could see a black handkerchief shoved into his back left pocket, along with a slingshot. I wasn't sleepy anymore. I turned to a new page in my notebook and began to write. Back then, I carried a journal everywhere. It was filled with little sketches and accounts of my days. I was worried about forgetting. I must have been really into my writing, because I looked up and there he was, standing over me, with a smirk on his face and those green eyes of his sparkling like stars. Pan had his milkshake in hand, cap back on his head. He sat down at my table without asking permission. I pushed my fries toward him. I knew that I would give him anything before I even knew his name.

Pan took me to Neverland that night. I didn't know what to expect. It was not the first time I'd played these games, but this—this was different. There was no fucking, no build toward something as simple as sexual release. He cut me. He took his knife from its leather holster and traced it across my throat. I didn't know this powerful boi. Everything about my world then was dangerous. I knew danger, tasted it on my dry morning lips and held it at bay from my hiding spot in the shadows as the grownups rushed to and from their offices. I was as friendly with danger as I was with uncertainty, but as Pan's knife trailed across my body, I was actually afraid. It was the first time in a very long time I felt anything. He came up behind me and whispered in my ear:

"Boi, to call Neverland home, you must wear our sign, two stars on your right shoulder."

I turned to face him and he pulled his shirt off before turning away from me. Above his Ace bandage I saw two stars scarred into his shoulder. I looked at the clean lines and shivered.

"I will wear your stars with pride," I replied and pulled off my grimy T-shirt.

Pan laid me down on a rough wooden bench. I flinched as he pulled off my binder but didn't resist. It was freezing in Neverland, yet his hands were warm as they felt the muscles in my shoulder. He traced the shape of two stars with the cold, wet ink of a permanent marker.

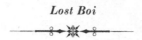

"You sure you want to be mine, boi? Do you swear to never grow up?" Pan growled.

"Yes, Sir!" I had never really belonged to anyone before. I was ready. I came alive, and I became his. I had no idea what I was consenting to or how deep the knife went, but I wanted more.

Pan led me, raw skin and oozing wounds, to a hammock, my hammock. The other lost bois had already put my pack under it, knowing that he was jumping me in and that I would be staying. I can't remember their names—bois came and went so fast, and if you stayed long enough, you learned that Pan was right: anyone who left wasn't worth a memory. That night, I was high on him, on the world he promised me, gazing at the faint glow of stars through the city haze and filthy windows. I got to belong to someone, and not just any someone—I got to belong to Pan. It's all I'd ever wanted. Pan was good to me, took me in, claimed me. He taught me to battle. He was also strict, demanding, and utterly unpredictable. You never knew when he would tell us bois to go out and dumpster for dinner, but really what he meant was that we should blacken his boots. Everything was always adventure. It was hard to stay scared or sad for very long.

Runaway! Runaway!

This wasn't all Pan's doing. Wendi might have looked sweet, but she knew she wove powerful spells with her stories. These spilled onto paper late at night when the Darlings thought her asleep and then shot from her drugstore-pink lips on the open mic stage. The way Pan told it, he'd just wanted to hear how the story about the princess ended. It was the stories that made him secretly follow her home that night, for Wendi didn't see Pan and Erebos trail her down sidewalks and through back alleys back to 14 London Street.

Pan later told me that he almost turned around then, seeing that she lived in such a nice house. It sat in the middle of an average suburban neighbourhood at the corner of Kensington Avenue and London Street. Money was tight, but the Darlings had done well for themselves, and the house with the manicured yard that Mr Darling mowed on Sunday afternoons was their prized possession, the proof that they were respectable community members. It was everything that Pan hated. It was almost enough to make him walk away from a pretty grrrl, but then on the mailbox he read "The Darlings' Home For Girls," and he knew his plan would work.

Pan watched Wendi go into the house, and a few minutes later a light came on upstairs. He left Erebos on the ground and climbed a tree that reached to the second storey. Then he waited. He should probably have felt a little creepy watching through the window as Wendi undressed, but he enjoyed the show. He didn't mean anything disrespectful—he never analyzed pleasure, just appreciated it. Wendi's room was tidy and organized, with light-pink walls and books neatly lining the shelves. Black-and-white photo-booth strips and concert tickets precisely arranged to look haphazard were taped to the mirror of the white vanity that stood next to her bed. The room looked like a clipping from a decorating magazine. Only the two kids, with their ragged edges, were out of place in this pretty little room. Watching Wendi slip into her nightgown and comb her long, dark brown hair, Pan wanted to take her away, to show her another world. Erebos had fallen asleep at the foot of the tree, and Pan's feet were tingling, but still he waited. Finally, the nightlights went out, and only then did he creep to the window ledge and into the room.

Pan had been surprised to see John Michael, and for a moment thought Wendi had a boyfriend, or a boi. Then, he remembered the group-home sign out front. Later, he told me how he'd almost walked away when he heard Wendi wish John Michael goodnight. Whatever their relationship was, it was clear they were a package deal. But what is one more boi? Especially if that deal is sweetened by a grrrl. John Michael must have been a deep sleeper, because she later swore that she never stirred as Pan cracked the window open and slipped past her bed, but the rustling of feathers and Pan's tears (that he will always deny having shed) woke Wendi.

Tink, of course, had followed Pan all the way to Wendi's and flown into the bedroom. Then, finding herself trapped inside the room, she began to panic, throwing herself into the walls, looking for the window. Tink crashed into a framed poster of white kittens and disappeared behind a dresser. Pan, convinced Tink was dead, couldn't keep from crying. The sound woke Wendi, who switched on her bedside lamp and gasped when she saw Pan standing at the foot of her bed, more alive than in the dream she'd just awoken from.

Tink would peck my eyes out if she thought I'd gotten this far into the story without properly introducing her. Tink is Pan's fairy. Unlike loyal and obedient Erebos, Tink is a jealous creature. Pigeons are so small that, unlike dogs, they can only hold one emotion at a time, and with Tink it is usually not a very nice one. Especially if there is a grrrl involved. She wants to be the only grrrl in Pan's life. When she gets into a mood, there's no reasoning with her, and no reminding her that she's a bird and no one will take her place. I see that confused look. Fairy? Pigeon? There is magic everywhere around you, but most people are too busy being grownup to notice it.

I'm not sure how Pan first met the pigeons; they must have been the feral ones nesting in the rafters of Neverland. Back before Pan was leader of the lost bois, he was alone with no one to talk to except for the pigeons. It didn't take long for them to adopt him into the flock. When a boi is brought into Neverland, he is given a pigeon. It's part of how you know that you're home, and it means you're never alone.

Starting when they hatch, us bois keep the fairies close, so they know how to find us. Sometimes, they follow us out on our adventures. Pan taught us how to make small leather leg bands for the pigeons, where their names can be embossed. Tink wears a green leather band around her ankle that matches the thick leather cuffs Pan makes for each of his lost bois and locks onto our wrists the day we swear our loyalty to him and to the principles of Neverland, the most important of which is, of course, to never grow up. I'll never forget the day that I met my pigeon, Washington. He had the most brilliant purple blaze of feathers right above his wings. When Pan handed him to me, I was nervous. I'd never held a bird before, and I certainly never thought I would hold a filthy pigeon. I held out my hand, palm up, and he hopped onto it. I thought my heart might break out of my chest as Washington fluttered and found his footing on my arm in our new home. The grownups' army used to use pigeons, but people have forgotten how smart they are. They learn where home is and, magically, they can always find their way back. We send messages to each other tucked into special little leather harnesses we made to fit each of them.

Anyway, Tink appeared from behind the dresser, feathers askew, but still very much alive. Relieved that Tink wasn't hurt, but knowing how jealous she would be, Pan sent her out of Wendi's bedroom window into the stars and back to Neverland to tell us bois that he would be home soon. Pan had been gone all day, and he knew we would worry that the Pirates had got him tied up and he might forget to come home to us. Pan's message just said that he was on his way home, not that he was bringing a grrrl. That's where the trouble started, but here I am getting ahead of myself again.

"Boi, you don't have to cry," Wendi whispered. She was now sitting up in her little bed. She let the pale pink comforter slip away, revealing her thigh. Had Pan been paying attention, he would have seen the cross-hatching of pink and red slashes. Her respectably coral-tipped nails toyed with the buttons of her nightgown at her throat, and she slowly began to undo them in a way that almost looked accidental. Again she whispered, "Boi, what's wrong?"

Pan rubbed his tattooed knuckles across his wet eyes, drying them on the tattered and frayed cuff of his green sweatshirt. Face twisted into his most charming smile, he turned and whispered in his husky voice, "I've come to hear the end of the story."

Wendi stalled, wanting to know more about this stranger she'd been fantasizing about. She licked her lips and pulled her hair up into a bun, a gesture that revealed the curve of her breasts under the clingy white nightgown, sticky with sweat in the warm spring night. Whispering so as not to wake John Michael, she patted the mattress next to her and tried to ask him the kinds of questions grownups ask. Wendi was not a grownup, but even then she was the kind of grrrl who could turn at any moment.

She made the mistake of first asking about mothers—that is, about his. She should have known better, being a foster child, but her world was so straight back then. I can picture how Pan must have prickled at that question. He told her coldly that he found mothers to be overrated sorts of persons. Wendi pushed when Pan said he had no last name, when he told her that "Pan" was the only name he had. If it had been me, I would have gone back out the window. Wendi was a good grrrl, always on the honour roll, with plans for going to college. Even though she didn't have them, she was convinced that everyone *should* have parents, or at the very least want them. Wendi believed that no matter how badly the grownups had treated her, they could be good. It had never occurred to her that she didn't have to become one.

Finally, after not getting useful answers out of Pan, Wendi asked him where he lived. Pan's eyes glittered as they always did when he talked about Neverland, about us bois. He told her that we had our own warehouse, a paradise we were always working on, patching the shot-out windows, hanging swings and slings, and about the day we added hammocks for each of us to sleep in amongst the rafters with our pigeons. Pan told Wendi he had a pack of bois who jumped at his command, who had sworn themselves to him and wore his cuff. He told her we too loved stories.

I don't know exactly what Pan promised Wendi in that little pink bed. Probably nothing more than adventure, with his crooked grin and the way his eyes twinkled when he talked about the things they could do together, but he locked a leather cuff around her wrist that night. It had been enough for me; there was no reason to think it wouldn't have been enough for her. Later, Wendi said that he told her about grrrls, how there weren't any of them in the Neverland, and how lonely that made him, us. How there was something special about a grrrl like her, something she could give him, us. Pan talked of how we would cherish and worship her, how she would always care for and feed her bois. "I love the way you talk about grrrls," Wendi whispered through glossed lips, placing her hand on Pan's denim thigh. She tried for a kiss, but Pan was already distracted, looking out the window to check on Erebos. Pan didn't want a grrrlfriend, he wanted a Mommy to tuck him in and put him in his place, but he would never have said that last part.

After fantasizing about this mysterious boi for weeks, only to have him appear in her bedroom, there was no question in Wendi's mind that she would go. She took her homework out of her backpack and filled it instead with dresses, drugstore lipstick, nail polish, and her notebook. Then she woke John Michael. I don't know if she had really been asleep, because it doesn't seem like she took much convincing to pack her own bag and follow Pan and Wendi out the window. Pan really had no need for more bois, but Wendi wouldn't leave her behind. Pan was so eager to have Wendi, he quickly consented to the tag-along.

The Adventure

Climbing down the tree had been hard for everyone except Pan. Wendi and John Michael tried and failed to imitate Pan's controlled free-fall from the branches. Wendi later told me that while she liked the way Pan had talked about grrrls, he didn't know how to treat a lady. As Wendi's foot left the window ledge, Pan was already on the ground, and he was playing with Erebos as Wendi fell. It never occurred to him to extend a hand to help her down; he was used to us bois. Wendi picked herself up from the grass, adjusted her bun, and straightened her nightgown. John Michael had fallen behind her in a painful tangle of elbows and knees. By the time she reached Neverland, she had a delicious shiner. While Wendi tied her little white canvas flats, John Michael steadied herself against the pull of Pan grabbing her hands behind her back. He leaned in and whispered, "You're my lost boi now," and locked a green leather cuff onto her wrist. Pan led them over the back fence and into the alley. The Darlings, meanwhile, were sitting at the dining room table working on their budget and didn't even notice the children were gone.

Pan led them away from the house through a dizzying maze of back alleys. He didn't dare go onto the streets, knowing that at any moment they could be spotted. Pan had shown many a boi how to fly away through an open window, how to disappear in the night and never be found. The Darlings' house sits far from the edge of city, near suburbia, so it was quite a journey back to Neverland. Wendi and John Michael wanted to take the bus, but Pan wasn't sure it was safe. Those two looked like runaways, even if the kids (as he was coming to think of them) hadn't a clue about how green they looked—and, given the hour, how easily they could be picked up. Pan paused and looked at them in the glow of a streetlight. Wendi wore a baby-pink hoodie covering that white nightgown he wanted into. Even the boi John Michael in her sweatpants looked like she had stepped off a school softball field, and her purpling eye made the group look even more suspicious. Pan took them through a hole in a chain-link fence into the darkness of a small stand of trees, wondering how long it would take for them to look crusty enough to not arouse suspicion.

The kids tried to keep up with Pan and Erebos as they skidded down a gravel hill and onto the train tracks. They were worried now, the reality of having climbed out their window beginning to sink in as their sneakers slid on the gravel beside the tracks. There was a freeway to their left about fifty feet up a hill, and the streetlight provided a grimy blanket of light—not enough to make sense of the details of where they were, but enough to keep an eye on the railroad ties and keep from slipping into the ditch. Pan warned them to stay to the shadows, but otherwise didn't talk for a while. There was enough light for Wendi to look at John Michael. She could see fear in the pale face of this boi whom she had come to think of as her little brother. Even that night on the train tracks, before she came to Neverland, Wendi was aware of the power she wielded and the responsibility she had, and now she shivered with the realization that she was leading John Michael astray. She knew that the boi looked up to her, trusted her, and relied upon her. Since coming to the Darlings' home, Wendi had rushed through her own home-work so she could help John Michael with hers. Now, Wendi focused on her excitement, fingering Pan's leather cuff on her wrist and pulling down her sleeve to protect it. She pushed away the fear that she was being irresponsible, that she was ruining the future she'd worked so hard for. She needed Pan; that's all she knew for certain.

There was a wildness to Pan that Wendi hadn't noticed at the bookstore. He was feral, she was sure of that now. The wild of him should have scared her back to roads with side-walks and bright streetlights and her warm, pink bed, but instead she followed him further into his world. The only part of the city Wendi had known until now was the bookshop where she read, and the diner down the block where, when the Darlings permitted her a later curfew, she would go and sit with the baby dykes from her GSA, talking poetry. They would eat fries and sip coffee that was really equal parts sugar and milk, just as they imagined grownups did.

As they walked further from 14 London Street, Pan slowly began to open up about the world he was bringing them into. It occurred to him only then, after he'd taken Wendi, that he hadn't told her or John Michael enough about us and the way we lived. He told them that Neverland was a special place, a whole world full of wonder built out of the things that no one else wanted, the treasures that grownups couldn't see, just like the bois who built it. Pan told them about the art room where we'd spray-painted murals of deep forests on two of the walls and blue undersea scenes on the others, the floor a muddy mix of colour and dirt where the paint of the two scenes meet. Pan told them about the hammocks where we slept and the piles of rope for suspending other things. He told them that if they wanted to, they could fly. Then, without explaining anything more, he said that no matter what, they would become his.

Pan doesn't do cultural competency trainings, and he doesn't do 101. He thinks that's for wusses and assimilationists. That's one of the things he and Hook never agreed about, but I'm getting ahead of myself again. Pan did not ask John Michael or Wendi for a safe word. He simply explained how things work. Neverland is a paradise, his paradise, and it runs by Pan's rules, and his alone. Pan explained, as they walked along the tracks, that Wendi and John Michael had to swear their allegiance to him, as all of us had once done. In return, he would care for them, and he promised that they would always be well used. John Michael, who was not inexperienced with sex games, quickly realized that this was more than that, much more complicated. Her hands were sweating as her mind raced. "Yes, Pan ..." she finally muttered.

Pan stopped walking and turned to her. The gold in his green eyes, glistening in the dim light, met hers for the first time, and she understood how deep this all would go. "Yes, what." It was not a question.

"Yes, Sir," John Michael replied, her face glowing red.

John Michael later told me she couldn't believe her luck. She'd been reading books about kinky protocol that Wendi would bring home from the queer bookstore, and suddenly there was this boi who appeared in her bedroom, living all the things she'd only read about. Best of all, he wanted her!

Wendi always says she lost track of how long she had been walking, but remembered noticing the scenery on either side of the tracks had changed from Interstate and sparse trees to buildings, mostly old and seemingly abandoned. She shortened the distance between herself and Pan, feeling safer in his shadow. Her eyes fixed on Erebos's tail as she darted ahead, leading the way toward Neverland. Wendi was grateful it was so dark, for she was certain she flushed with embarrassment and desire as Pan explained to John Michael that, though

Wendi now wore his cuff, she was also to be his Mommy and Mommy to all his bois.

Like John Michael, Wendi was less innocent than she appeared. The stories at the open mic had convinced Pan of that. She understood the basics of D/s and leather, and had even experimented with grrrlfriends, but never... How do I say this politely, dear reader? She didn't fancy herself a switch, let alone any sort of Top, or a person of authority over another. For the first time, language failed her. Mommy/boi, Wendi realized, is what this adventure would be called, but could she be a Mommy? And then it occurred to her that everything she had done with those old grrrlfriends had been a child's game of make-believe, and what she was about to embark upon was deeper than where she had been before. Pan told her that he played for keeps when he closed the cuff around her wrist. For a moment, it seemed as though he was going to extend his hand to her, but then it came to rest on Erebos's head instead. Wendi looked away, trying to ignore the hot sting of tears.

They walked for a long time in silence. She did not think once about the Darlings. Wendi and John Michael were getting tired. It was far past their bedtime, and the initial excitement of having run away was beginning to wear off. They were each lost in thought, imagining the adventures they would have or the trouble that could come when their departure was discovered. Their thoughts drifted to less accepting homes they had been placed in and the fear that they would

be sent back to them, or worse, cast out on their own. They
realized that now they were alone, and they needed Pan.
When he spoke, they jumped at the sound of his voice breaking through the night, sounding like a lifetime of cigarettes.

Pan pointed to a trail of smoke on the other side of the
fence. They could hear chanting and drumming drifting like
the smoke into the night air. "That's the Urban Primitives,"
Pan whispered. "I don't like them."

John Michael had heard of them. "I don't give a fuck what
kind of spiritual meaning they think they're getting," she said.
"That's stolen ritual, and they have no right to it! Goddamn
racists, could they be any more colonialist?" John Michael
whispered through clenched teeth.

All of this talk irritated Pan. He didn't like the Urban
Primitives. They were sworn enemies of the lost bois because
they were a bunch of racist pricks, and he personally took
pleasure in letting the air out of their bike tires whenever he
saw them parked outside of the organic food co-op. But he
mostly hated that John Michael already knew of them; he
always wanted to be the one who knew everything.

Pan grew quiet again as they kept walking. The train tracks
had taken a steady turn to the right. Wendi could smell
rotting fish and hear water lapping down the hill from the
tracks. "That," said Pan, pointing to what appeared to be a
floating house, "is the Lagoon, where the Mermaids live."

Wendi squinted into the dark and could make out the shape
of a little red house with black trim that seemed to be sitting

right on the water. It was old and looked as though someone had just thrown it into a puddle. The roof was sagging, and there were no handrails on the second-floor widow's walk. She couldn't make herself look away until she tripped over a broken bottle and would have fallen if John Michael hadn't reached out to steady her.

"Who are the Mermaids?" Wendi whispered to Pan, again trying to catch his hand. Pan puffed up, eager to have the power that knowledge once again restored to him. "The Mermaids," Pan explained, "are a gang of femmes—they're not girls."

I once watched a new boi make that mistake. Before the word "girl" even finished falling out of his unfortunate mouth, Undine had thrown him up against the wall of Neverland with her little silver knife pressed to his throat. All I could see was her teal Bettie Page hair and the way her knuckles tightened around the mother-of-pearl knife handle. The boi never made that mistake again.

Pan told Wendi that the Mermaids are our biggest allies, that they are beautiful and fierce and incredibly loyal, mostly to each other. He told her that they are nocturnal, working the streets and the bars by the Interstate, pleasing men. With that he hocked a loogie and spat over the edge of the tracks. Wendi couldn't hear it hit the water below, but she watched it fall like a dirty, snotty falling star.

Pan didn't speak for a moment, but sensing Wendi's impatience, began again. "There are six Mermaids now living in that house, though the number ebbs and flows like the dirty water. Now it's Siren, the leader, Undine, Melusine, Naiad, Ningyo, and Kelpie. They are, as I said, most loyal to each other, sharing their earnings to make the rent on the houseboat and filling it with as much finery as they can. Before you think them shallow and materialistic, you should know how hard they work for every stitch of dress, and they steal their makeup from the drugstore—but that's another story. The Mermaids work harder than anyone I've ever met, and are the most creative too. They dumpster at the university behind the art building, finding bolts of fabric and rolls of ribbon, which they transform into curtains for each window on the little house and string like billowing walls to create private sleeping caverns in the little attic."

Pan didn't tell Wendi about the Mermaids' dirty little secret, but I guess he spared her ours too. He didn't mention the liquor bottles thrown into the river from the attic window, the SOS message of dirty needles. Pan didn't know it, but Wendi would figure out soon enough that the Crocodile was always after them. The Mermaids liked to think that the Crocodile was their friend, that they had tamed it, and it protected them against their work, against those men. The Mermaids were always making bargains and deals, but the Crocodile always took their money and swam away, leaving them dazed and confused. After all, heroin is heroin no matter what you call it. You can't domesticate a monster.

The Mermaids are our biggest allies, but they are separate

from us. Pan makes sure of that. For all of his love of fluidity, there are lines he just won't let be crossed. A couple of years ago, right after I came to Neverland, there was a big fight between us and the Mermaids. It was the kind of fight that almost ruined everything about our alliance. Naiad broke some unwritten rule and asked Pan for his cuff. Instead of refusing her respectfully, he laughed, and she left Neverland in tears.

Naiad had been so good in the way that she had approached him. All winter, she'd been at Neverland, learning how to hold the pigeons and battle with us bois. She knew how to black boots, and her knees were as calloused as ours. She wore old ripped band shirts and a short skirt with her combat boots. Naiad was a femme, but a boi too, and she wanted to leave the Lagoon and become Pan's boi. All winter, he led Naiad on, letting her battle and dumpster with us. We saw her as one of us, but everything changed the night that she was alone with Pan, us bois in our hammocks listening in. Siren later told me that Naiad had prepared for this moment for months, talked of nothing else. The other Mermaids knew that she wanted to be a lost boi, secure in her place under Pan's boot.

Pan must have known what was coming, but he was going to make her come out and say it. He cleared his throat.

"You wanted to speak with me?"

"Yes, Sir," Naiad replied firmly.

Silence.

"Sir, all winter I have been with your bois, learning the way you like your coffee and how you prefer your boots done. I can hold my own in a battle as well as any boi. Sir, all I want is to join your pack, to be one of your lost bois."

We heard a thud that could only be a boi falling to her knees, and then ... the horrible sound of Pan's cruellest laugh. Maybe at first he thought that Naiad was playing, but when she fell to her knees, he must have known she was serious. He laughed anyway.

"No grrrls allowed," he finally said.

It seemed unlike him—after all, he'd fought against Hook's Old Guard rigidity, and yet Pan couldn't see the boi trembling before him, a boi who believed in magic and who was ready to take an oath never to grow up and to serve him loyally. But Pan couldn't or wouldn't see her. Naiad was left to peel herself off the cold, pigeon-shit-covered concrete as Pan's attention turned to some scraps of leather. But that was long ago.

Wendi and John Michael kept walking behind Pan, and only he knew that they were getting close to Neverland. A flock of pigeons burst from the broken windows on the upper floor of a warehouse, and Wendi gasped.

Pan only laughed. "That" he said, "is Neverland." But instead of leading them directly to us, he pointed to a hole in the fence on the other side of the tracks, and led them into an alley. "This is the Jolly Roger, home to Hook and his Pirates. You need to see that first."

Pan told them that the Pirates were almost worse than grownups, because they knew better; they knew the life they could have had, but instead pledged their service to Hook, the worst of all. Wendi could feel something in the way that Pan talked of Hook, but she couldn't guess what it meant. Pan then turned and pointed to a little window, almost completely hidden by a dumpster. "Want to have an adventure?" his crooked grin teased. For a moment, Wendi thought of how wrong it was to trespass, but then she reminded herself that she was a runaway who had only hours before given her consent to Mommy a boi who was probably twice her age. This was not a night for logic. This was a night for breaking rules. They slipped through the window into darkness. Wendi looked back longingly at the sidewalk and the warm glow of the street lamp. Pan hit a switch, and electric wall-mounted candles flickered on, illuminating a room with burgundy walls. Suddenly Wendi recognized the smell that had punched her as soon as they crawled through the window. There was more leather here than either she or John Michael had ever seen—furniture, benches, platforms, and crosses made entirely of leather and steel filled the room. Between the flickering lights hung whips, floggers, cuffs, hoods, and things Wendi didn't know at all. There were beautiful coils of black rope labelled with the names Smee, Starkey, Jukes, and Cecco.

"Those belong to the Pirates," sneered Pan. "Hook takes safety to extremes; he doesn't know how to let go, how to be

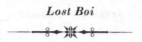
free. He says it's part of having 'good form.' Hook thinks he's Old Guard, and good form is everything to him," finished Pan.

"Good form?" Wendi hesitantly asked.

Pan grinned. "He's got rules for everything, and a high standard that he holds everyone, mostly himself, to. For Hook, good form is more than rules. It's how he constructs the world around him, the expectations he holds for himself and his Pirates. It's a code of conduct that he never breaks."

John Michael pulled cuffs off the wall, fingered the smooth stitching, and then put them back. Next, she grabbed one of the heavy oar-shaped paddles that hung suspended between pegs and playfully swung it toward Wendi. Turning his attention to John Michael, Pan whispered, "All bois in service to me must swear that Hook is always to be left to me. You may battle any of his Pirates in whatever way you please, black and blue if you want, but Hook is mine. Understood?"

"Mine" was such a strange word: As in Pan's lover? His enemy? Wendi didn't dare ask. She felt almost jealous of the way that Pan had called Hook his, but she didn't yet understand why. John Michael, eager to prove allegiance, responded with a convincingly quick "Yes, Sir."

The Jolly Roger is an old brownstone whose basement room has been restored and made to appear antique and elegant. While Pan talked to John Michael about Hook, Wendi inspected a wooden table carved with intricate ships and waves. She had been crouching to look more closely at a sailing ship so detailed you could see sailors on the tiny deck preparing the sails for the carved storm approaching. When she stood, her eyes met the gleam of steel. Arranged on the tabletop was an array of hooks, beautiful ones of fancy shining metal. In the back row was one of medium size, not as elaborate as the rest. The steel was polished to a shine, but it was otherwise almost ordinary in appearance. Next to it was a little black card, like the ones that had sat in front of the rope coils. In the same golden script, Wendi read the name: Pan.

"I ruined him." Pan's voice pulled Wendi back. Pan told the two of them how, years ago, Pan had thrown a piece of Hook to the Crocodile. They almost didn't believe him. John Michael didn't mean to be disrespectful, but until now, she hadn't fully understood the cruelty of the world they had just entered.

Wendi wanted to ask a question, but there was a sound outside the door, the unmistakable sound of heavy boots on stairs. Quickly Pan flicked off the light. John Michael had stashed herself under a table, but Wendi stupidly stood frozen. Pan pushed her toward the window.

"I'll meet you at Neverland!" His hoarse whisper echoed in her ears as she ran. "Second streetlight on the right and straight on till Morning Street," was all Pan told Wendi about how to get to Neverland. He purposely didn't give her enough information to find Neverland; he didn't yet trust her, but at that moment, Wendi trusted him completely.

Hook's Dirty Truth

ithout Pan around, things at Neverland were usually quiet. It's like the magic just evaporated when he was away. Sometimes us bois would stage battles with each other, but usually there was more than enough of that when Pan was home, so when he went out on one of his adventures, we tended to keep to ourselves. It was hard to find joy in anything when Pan wasn't with us. Sometimes we talked about the past, or what we could remember of it, anyway, because birth families, and especially parents, were a forbidden topic when Pan was around. Most of us couldn't remember much of anything from before we fell out of our prams or were pushed out of them. We've all got reasons for having left our parents. I don't want to remember mine.

Mothers are the kind of grownups that Pan and I hate more than any others; I understood completely why Pan would forbid us from talking about them. This is where Slightly and I disagreed—she felt the need to flaunt her memories, all the good ones, anyway, the big family dinners, vacations to the beach, that kinda shit. Things didn't get bad for her until after her mother died. Cancer, I think. Slightly didn't like to talk about what came next, the group homes she had to live in because her perfect little extended family was too busy with their picket-fence lives to make room for an orphan. Slightly usually ignored that part of the story, and instead talked about her perfect mother and showed off her pink rosary beads. It's easy to make a saint out of someone who's gone. Slightly was so pretentious, always talking like she was better than us because she graduated high school and could have gone to college. It made me want to just punch her for not appreciating how lucky she was to be away in our own world. I never understand what Pan saw in her. There were six of us bois in Neverland before Wendi and John Michael arrived. The number of us bois could shift dramatically, because the world's a dangerous place. I mean, it wasn't uncommon for a boi to disappear—or die. If you're going to fall out of your pram, I guess that's just something that you have to get used to. There were also bois who couldn't hack it, who didn't meet Pan's expectations, who had to go. Neverland was the kind of place where we could be anything we wanted, everything we never believed was possible before we got lost. Pan would forgive his bois for pretty much anything, except growing up. It's harsh, but once a boi grows up, Pan just forgets he ever existed.

That horrible day when Wendi came, Siren and Kelpie were at Neverland. Pan had told Kelpie that he would take her out to the roller derby. He knew the dyke working the door, and she had promised to let them in for free. Kelpie is a big femme who cuts the crotch out of her fishnet stockings to help them fit over her thick thighs and, let's be real, to save time. She's kinda the closest thing that Pan's ever had to a grrrlfriend. Kelpie danced at the peep-show place by the Interstate, and Pan liked to surprise her at the end of her shift, when she traded stilettos for boots and threw her bleach-stiffened pink hair into pigtails. Kelpie is tough, but her face always softened into a smile when she pushed open the heavy black door, stepped into the alley behind the club, and saw Pan leaning against a dumpster. He never told her that he was coming, but luckily for him, she never had plans that couldn't be ditched for milkshakes and fries at the all-night diner. Kelpie was tender and soft with Pan in a way she couldn't be with anyone else. She told him things, let him touch her in a way that no one else could. Kelpie was close to all us bois; she respected us and our role in Pan's life, but she also wanted more than Pan could give. The week before Wendi arrived, Kelpie'd asked Pan if he would start calling her his grrrlfriend.

Siren and I had been messing around together for a few months, at that point. Mostly, we saw each other when Pan wasn't around. Its not that we bois weren't allowed to hook up, it's just that Pan preferred that us bois kept our external entanglements simple, so that our primary focus was on service to him. Sometimes he had to help us, to forbid us from seeing someone. I was always grateful when that happened, because it helped me to keep my focus on what mattered most.

Siren and Kelpie were as close as Pan and I were, and so when Kelpie and Pan were going to meet up at Neverland to go on their date, Siren tagged along. All afternoon, Kelpie waited for Pan to show up. Siren and I tried to keep her occupied with stories and snacks, but as evening stretched into night, she finally gave up. Kelpie pulled on her boots, reapplied her lip gloss, and went into the bathroom, emerging a few moments later with eyes glazed and far away, tugging the sleeves of her shirt down quickly. Siren offered to go to the roller derby with her, out of Mermaid solidarity, but Kelpie refused, saying that she was going to bike up to the arena. Not twenty minutes after she left, I was lying on the floor on an old sleeping bag with Siren when Tink flew in through the jagged glass of a broken window. Siren had just reapplied her cherry lipstick and lit a cigarette. Curled up on the sleeping bag wearing only stockings and a lacy bra, Siren was ready to pounce. I groaned as Tink pecked me hard while I struggled to get Pan's letter out of her harness.

Bois—
On my way to Neverland. Be ready to present yourselves.
Have two new hammocks prepared.
—Pan

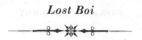
As I read the note, Tink soared to the rafters to sulk. I
threw the crumpled paper down next to me and groaned.
Siren looked so beautiful—I mean she always does, but I
don't think she believed that, no matter how many times I
told her. As she read Pan's note, her face went hard. She didn't
like that Pan had stood up Kelpie, that he seemed to have
forgotten about her entirely, and for what? More bois? As
she stared at the letter, I thought about the way the black
slip she wore rode up her fishnet-covered thighs and how the
toes of her black boots would get jammed into the chain-link
fence that surrounds Neverland when she climbed it. When
we fucked, I would fantasize about licking those boots, but
she'd never let me. Siren wanted a boifriend, not a boi. I didn't
know what I wanted.

Siren saw her first. I looked out the window and was surprised to see a grrrl struggling to climb that chain-link fence.
She was such a silly looking little grrrl, wearing a pink hoodie
and a white nightgown, with bare legs and little white sneakers. I glanced behind me; Siren was already pulling her black
slip-dress over her head and lacing her boots tight against
the curve of her calves. I didn't know what to do. I could
have called the other bois; it's what I should have done, but I
didn't want to look weak in front of Siren. I guess I actually
looked pretty helpless, because she rolled her eyes, took one
last drag of her cigarette, threw it into a nearby beer can, and
stood. "You going to just sit there with your cock out and let
Neverland be invaded?"

I blushed and pulled hard enough to get my cock out of
its harness, then threw it up into my hammock. Standing, I
zipped my jeans, thankful I hadn't taken my boots off. I followed Siren out of the room and into our makeshift kitchen.
It has a view of the fence, and we could see Wendi trying to
pick her way over the barbed wire. Siren laughed and pulled
another cigarette out of her purse. I fumbled for my lighter
but was too slow. Siren's chipped red nails flicked the little
silver-and-pearl box. She cupped her hand around the flame
and took a sharp inhale, then stashed the lighter back into
her bra.

"Grrrls that clean are always trouble, and not the good
kind. She's ether a spy, preparing to snitch on us, or she's
going to bring bad luck." Siren managed to laugh and be serious at the same time. I didn't ask how she knew about grrrls
like that.

"What should we do?" I asked. Siren blew a smoke ring; I
wished my cock wasn't in the hammock. Siren said that Pan
would want me to protect Neverland, that he would want me
to take charge, confront this pretty little grrrl and tell her that
either she could get jumped in or she had to go. Everything
Siren said made sense, and more than anything I wanted Pan
to be proud of me. I looked up and saw that the grrrl had
made it down the fence and was now crawling through a
broken window. She yelped as her ankle caught a shard of
broken glass, and her shoe was spattered with red.

Tink had come to roost on Siren's shoulder and pulled

a syringe and baggie from her purse as the grrrl climbed through that window and saw us standing there. I admired how she held my gaze when she first saw me, but when she looked down, Siren fired a series of questions at her without letting her answer.

"Hey, pretty grrrl, who are you? What's your name? How did you get here? Why aren't you talking? Who sent you? You're a snitch spy, aren't you? That's why you aren't talking, isn't it?"

After whispering her name, the grrrl didn't even try to answer Siren's questions. When Siren told her to get the fuck out, Wendi fell to her knees before me and began to sob and sputter. "Don't make me go! Please don't send me away."

Confused, I looked to Siren, who just rolled her eyes. When I looked again at Wendi, I saw that her long, dark hair had fallen from its bun and stuck to the sweat on her face and beautiful throat. I'd never had a grrrl kneeling in front of me. My stomach lurched, and I couldn't tell if I was going to cum or puke.

"Please, what do you want?" she whispered from glossy pink lips. I looked at the gash on her ankle, the way the blood had beaded. Siren started to laugh.

"If this grrrl wants us to believe she's not some sort of snitch, then she has to prove it. She has to swim with the Crocodile." I knew that this strange grrrl couldn't know what she was consenting to. But then I thought of Pan. I thought of how proud he would be of me if I, in his absence, protected

Neverland. I left her on the floor and sat at the dumpstered table with Siren.

This was not the first time that Neverland had been discovered by an outsider. Every couple of years, it seemed, some poser kids would sneak in or befriend Pan and worm their way inside. It never took long for them to be discovered as frauds, but it was always a great nuisance, and dangerous too, because grownups could have followed them here, maybe even parents, the worst kinds of grownups, the ones who have the ability to destroy everything for all of us.

That was why I didn't question Siren when she said, "What would Pan do? Remember, he fed Hook to the Crocodile. I bet he would want you to shoot this pretty grrrl up, to jump her in." Siren's words rang true, and I was not the kind of boi to question Pan.

By now we weren't alone. News has a way of travelling fast in Neverland, in part on account of the lack of walls. Us bois are always climbing over each other; Pan likes it that way. He doesn't like to be alone, and I'm pretty sure that's why he has us bois in the first place. There isn't much privacy at Neverland. A grrrl, especially one who had broken in, was more than any of the bois could resist. They had all gathered around the little table, watching me and Wendi, who still knelt, silently pleading as delicious tears trailed her rounded cheeks. I can't imagine what Wendi thought of me, of us, a tangle of dirty denim, leather, ink, and steel shoved through various appendages. We all wore the same thrift-store workpants, and whatever T-shirts, hoodies, and flannels fit us best from the pile of clothes that lived in the corner of the sleeping room. None of us had anything of our own, except for Pan's cuff, and that belonged to him and not to us. I don't think Wendi had ever seen bois like us. We weren't like those guys at the GSA spouting "born in the wrong body" bullshit stories. All she could see was a pack of bois ready to take her down, and Siren reapplying her lipstick.

Wendi's eyes darted from boi to boi, studying us. Nibs was the dandiest one of us, always trying to get us to fold our clothes and reminding us to shower. Slightly was a strange boi whom Pan pulled from a bus stop where she'd been left slouched over and overdosing on ecstasy after a rave. She sobered up and decided to stay. Slightly and I didn't get along all that well, though we were forbidden from ever really having it out with each other. Curly was handy to have around because he enjoyed punishment and would always take the fall for things, even when he didn't do them. When Pan was in a mood, Curly was always the first to volunteer himself for punishment—greedy pig of a boi. Of course, this sometimes backfired on us, because Pan is anything but stupid, and while he loves to punish a boi, he is (at times) a fair leader and prefers (when possible) to punish the boi who deserved it. When he caught us, we were given a lashing twice: first, for not having volunteered and second, for letting another boi take the punishment that we should have been grateful to receive. The Twins must have had a particularly troubled past, because they fell from their pram together, and have never left each other. They even slept in the same hammock. Pan used to punish them for it.

All this time, as Wendi's eyes darted from boi to boi, I struggled with how best to defend Neverland. I didn't know yet that Pan was on an adventure hidden in the Pirate's dungeon with John Michael or that he meant this grrrl to be our Mommy.

Later, John Michael whispered to us bois about the rest of her adventure with Pan, how he'd motioned for John Michael to remain quiet. But from her place under the table, all she could make out was her face reflected in the toes of the immaculate boots that paced the room. Hook, Pan had told her, was Old Guard impeccable. John Michael hadn't known exactly what that meant, but she started to get an idea when his crew entered and presented themselves for inspection against the back wall.

Each crew member stood before Captain Hook, erect and in proper uniform, ready to be judged. He had carefully instructed his crew in the ways of the Pirates, and as he inspected them—tucking in a shirt here, adjusting a collar there, and shaking his head at a scuffed boot—he lectured them.

"A leather Pirate must always be respectable. He must present himself perfectly, always, in clothing and action. Black boots must always be worn. Do not mix different colours of leather; only black leather is appropriate. My crew will never

wear shorts, and should always wear denim or leather. Once earned, a Pirate should only be seen in his leather jacket. Only I, as your Captain, may wear a cap. Never wear the leather of another Pirate, unless it has been given to you.

"You are my crew because you wear my collar; you are mine, and mine alone. You are not to engage in battle of any kind with another Captain. Battling with lost bois is, of course, permitted. No Captain will engage you because you wear my collar, which means you are owned, you are off-limits, and they will stay away from you, if they have been trained properly and know what's good for them. Captains do not take collars, ever. Never forget: we Pirates are a breed unto ourselves."

Of course, none of this was new for Hook's crew, but John Michael was mesmerized. Pan always said that this was shit that Hook had found on a website or something, but Hook swore he was Old Guard-trained in the dungeons of San Francisco before everyone had died. Hook said that the rules were literally beaten into him, and that was how he trained his crew. In his own way, like Pan and all us lost bois, Hook avoided growing up. He never had to have a grownup job but lived in a world of sexual outlaws, travelling from kink conference to kink conference, teaching his history and helping others to appropriately train their submissives. Hook not only trained others in the rules passed down to him from the great leather Pirates who'd come before, but he dedicated his life to their honour and made sure not one member of his crew ever forgot that. In that way, his world inside the Jolly Roger was like our Neverland, separate from the morality and the judgments and the expectations of adults.

But the Pirates are our enemies because they are rich yuppies. Their fridges were always full. But they were different from grownups, because they lived by their own rules. Rules, Hook maintained, ensured the keeping of good form, and Hook was at his most seductive when he spoke about the importance of good form. When I first met him, I thought it was just about the clothes. After all, he wore only black leather: boots, pants, cap, gloves, pajamas (Pan always added that last one, when he'd make us bois pee ourselves laughing as he imitated one of Hook's serious lectures). Hook's keys always jingled from his left belt loop. He always laughed at Pan's black hanky flagging; after all, Pan had no keys. But I have to admit that good form went deeper than clothes for Hook. Pan had already told John Michael about the Crocodile, and how Hook had never forgiven him for hooking him. Of course, Hook would cut anyone who called him weak, for to show weakness would be to dishonour himself, his crew, and all the great leather Pirates who had come before.

Pan later told me that he didn't know exactly why he had taken Wendi and John Michael to the Jolly Roger before bringing them to meet us and to see Neverland. He struggled too with how to explain what his relationship was to Hook. They had nasty, bloody battles that fed them both in ways they couldn't talk about. Hook's normal protocols for scene negotiation didn't apply to his battles with Pan. They played hard, and they played for blood, and they played past breaking. Hook never forgave Pan for hooking him on the Crocodile, and Pan never forgot the morning he came to on Hook's dungeon floor, sore and wrecked and unwilling to admit he'd been had. That very day, he led the Crocodile right to Hook; the man never saw it coming. Hook might have been sunk, but Pan was attached to the anchor. He couldn't ever make himself want to walk away from that Pirate.

"It's only a matter of time before you are gobbled up by it." John Michael was shocked by the sweetness of Smee's voice when she first heard it. Still quite attached to her lesbian identity and unable to gender the voice she now heard, John Michael wanted to know if it came from the sort of person that she would be allowed to find attractive. From under the table, all she could see was the cuffed denim ankle and the mirrored shine of Smee's boots.

Now, I'm going to leave Pan and John Michael at the Jolly Roger, since they are about to get tied up for a while, and tell you what happened at Neverland.

When Pan was away from Neverland, we were like a litter of puppies who got destructive when left alone and crawled all over each other the minute our master walked through the door. On the night that Wendi came, us bois were extra nervous and kept pacing and looking out the window, waiting for Erebos to bound in with Pan tumbling behind. It didn't matter that we were all together. Without him, I felt unsteady, as though I could be blown away at any moment and no one would know I'd ever existed. Wendi was on the floor before me, and the bois had all circled around, waiting to see what I would do with this strange, clean, spy grrrl. What if Siren was right and she really could destroy everything? Wendi didn't want to kneel there, I know that now. She wanted to hose us down, and do the filthy dishes that filled the utility sink in the corner and were stacked along the floor. I know now that she just wanted to patch the holes in our knees, and that she wasn't so innocent that she didn't know just how they had gotten there. Wendi wanted to tell us stories, to tuck us in, to pull our smoke-and-mildew-smelling sleeping bags up to our chins. She wanted to shoplift teddy bears for us from the thrift shop. Pan had promised her a pack of obedient boys who wanted a Mommy, not an ambush. I didn't know any of this.

While staring at the pink edges of a scar on Wendi's plump thigh, I knew that Siren's eyes were on me. Finally, when I could think of nothing else to do, no other way out, I cleared my throat and looked down at Wendi, avoiding her eyes and resting on the smooth inner bend of her elbow. I heard Siren whisper, "Shoot Wendi. Pan would want you to protect Neverland."

I grabbed the syringe from the table and pulled the black handkerchief from my back right pocket, using it to tie off the arm that Wendi held out to me. Her eyes were fixed on

Siren, her face screwed into an expression that was intended to appear fierce but looked like a pout. My ears filled with the bois' whispers and the rustling of pigeons above my head. I shot Wendi and she hit the filthy ground, cradling her arm. Wendi was drowning and could hear only the gnashing of crocodile fangs.

The Little Family

It was only after I'd done it that I realized my mistake. Siren was silent, and the bois' constant whispering had ceased. I'd wanted to protect Neverland, to make Pan proud of me, and there was no way I could have known that he wanted this grrrl, that he'd brought her here not only for himself but for us. My stomach somersaulted as I watched her puddle onto the floor. Wendi'd presented her right arm to me, but now, as she thrashed on the dirty floor amidst feathers and bird droppings, bottle caps and crumbs, the sleeve of her pink hoodie was pushed up on her left arm, and I saw the thin band of dark green leather. It was more delicate than the one I wore, but instantly I recognized the cuff. The other bois, who moments earlier had been egging me on, also saw and turned, teeth bared, circling me.

"How could you have done this?" Curly said, turning away from me and sitting on the floor next to Wendi. The Twins too were shaken, which translated to anger.

"I bet Pan was bringing us a Mommy!" said one Twin.

"She would have taken care of us, mended the holes in our knees, tucked us in!" said the second.

"Now you've ruined her!" the first one cried. A Mommy was something Pan had talked of, but always in abstract ways. I thought this Mommy business was just a story he and I would jerk off to. He'd told us that the Mommy he would find for us would be strict. She'd make us scrub behind our ears and wash our mouths out with soap when we were disrespectful. Domestic discipline wasn't something I'd ever given much thought to, but Pan had, and he sold us all on the magic of a Mommy's touch. Still, I never thought he'd send us one as a surprise.

Seeing the cuff changed everything. I was dizzy with the idea of how stupid I'd been not to look at her wrist before things got so out of control. Another boi in my position might have blamed Siren, but I just couldn't bring myself to hate her. It was my choice. Pan teaches us to be responsible for our actions. I started to cry and was too upset to care that everyone could see. Finally, I wiped my snotty face on my sleeve and whispered, "I used to dream of pretty femmes, that someday one would come to be our Mommy. In my dreams, I would fall to my knees and say, 'Mommy, please, please have this boi.' It was always such a beautiful dream, and she would take my face in her hands and smile. But now, when my Mommy finally came to Neverland, I shot her."

I couldn't believe I'd let the bois see me act so weak. I

rushed into our sleeping quarters. When Pan was away, I'd always been unofficially second-in-command. How could I have let him down like this? I found my messenger bag and threw some clothes into it. Siren came to check on me. As much as I wanted to be alone, there was something about Siren; she didn't want me to top her, and she didn't especially want to top me. I could be weak in front of Siren in a way I couldn't with the other bois, but it still scared me to let her see me like that. Siren started to kiss me, and I kissed her back because I didn't know what else to do. My tongue was coated with her sticky cherry lip gloss, and she tasted like cigarettes. I didn't want to kiss her, not now, not like this, but I didn't want to stop either. What I really wanted was for Pan to take me down, to make it all right, to punish and absolve me, to change what I'd done. Siren knew I was lost, and not just in a lost boi sort of way.

She told me that I could come back to the Lagoon for the night. I was shocked. It's against the Mermaids' house rules to bring someone home without consulting each other. "Sometimes, rules are made to be broken." Siren's words hung in the air around us.

I left Siren there and walked back into Neverland's main room, where Wendi still lay on the floor, surrounded by the bois. I started toward the windows when the bois tried to stop me, saying how much they didn't want me to go. Curly stood there looking like he might start to cry, and my first instinct was to comfort him, to make a plan, but I couldn't do anything but run. It wasn't just that I was terrified of Pan. Greater than my fear of Pan was this new fear of myself. What I've always cherished about being a lost boi, other than belonging to Pan, of course, was the chance to find and save the other broken and forgotten runaways, throwaways. It's all I've ever wanted, to help them not be alone. I never thought I'd be capable of hurting someone the way I'd just hurt Wendi. Then came the sound I'd been dreading. Pan was home, and there was no time to escape.

"Bois, I've returned!" His bellowing announcement echoed through Neverland. All the pigeons flew from their roosts and circled us, making Erebos leap into the air after them. Pan was distracted for a moment, which gave me time to signal to the bois that we needed to hide Wendi. We stood in a line before Pan, as he liked us to present ourselves, waiting. Siren had gone out the back through the high window, onto the dumpster, and out onto the tracks. I didn't blame her for wanting to get out of my mess. Pan looked confused; we're always so lonely without him that, when he comes in, we normally throw ourselves at him, knocking him down, forgetting protocol in a way that he loves. On the night that Wendi came, none of us bois moved.

"Bois! I have something exciting to share! I've brought us a Mommy! She's smart and beautiful the way a Mommy should be!" Pan always talked about Mommy play like other people talk about living full-time D/s, the way we do. It was like a fantasy, not something I thought would ever actually happen. I almost let myself get excited until I realized that I'd ruined everything. Neverland was silent; Pan looked at me.

I knew that most of the other bois would have continued to hide her, but I had to do right by my Sir. I waved my hand and the bois moved out of formation. When Pan first saw Wendi, she was lying so still that she looked dead. He looked at her, confused. I wanted to run to him, to assure him that she wasn't dead, but I wasn't sure, and he had knelt at her side.

"Wendi? Wendi?" His voice was high and shrill. "Oh, Wendi, don't be afraid. Death is dark, but don't be afraid to be dead, it's an adventure. But if you're not dead, please don't die! Mommy, come back!"

Pan saw the syringe lying next to him. "Whose?" was all he needed to say to put me back on my knees.

"Mine, Sir."

I hit the concrete floor without attempting to protect my knees. I wanted to hurt for him, for everything that I'd done to ruin our Mommy. The look on his face hurt me more than any punishment. It was a mixture of anger, betrayal, and something else I don't even know, maybe mourning for the dream he thought was finally going to come true.

Pan always carried with him, clipped to his belt, a little dagger shaped like an arrow, with a sharp point and a thin handle. He now raised the dagger above me. I didn't move, didn't cry. Instead, I laced my fingers behind my head, presented my chest to him, and prepared for the end. I felt proud of myself that I held true to everything he'd taught me, that

I didn't turn away. I faced what I had earned. Washington flew down from the rafters. Her feathers were fluffed and she perched herself on my shoulder, as if was going to peck Pan's eyes out if he moved any closer. The room was silent, except for Washington's distressed coos. As I knelt before Pan, I fought the urge to look away. I wanted to take my punishment honourably and with good form, so I kept my pitiful eyes locked on his. When Washington positioned herself on my shoulder, ready to attack, Pan made no motion toward her. He only raised one eyebrow. It was such a sexy, bemused look, and were the situation not so dire, I would have laughed and then thrown myself at his denim fly. Washington was such a loyal friend that she would've taken the blow for me, but I couldn't allow that. Only then did I break my eye contact with Pan. I took Washington from my shoulder and onto my hand. Meeting her small dark eyes, I hoped that my tears conveyed all the love I had for her. Then I lifted my arm and sent her away into the rafters. I wiped my eyes on my sleeve and raised them to again meet Pan's.

Pan raised his knife and prepared to strike but then dropped his hand to his side. Again, the knife was raised, but he could not stab me. At this moment, Wendi stirred out of her daze. She stood up and placed her hand on Pan's arm. A Mommy's first act. It's impossible to know if she had any idea of the power of her tiny hand resting on Pan's thick, tattooed forearm. I don't think she could have known the way that moment shifted time, and allegiance, even just a little.

I'd never seen anyone stand up to Pan, except for Hook, and that was only in battle. None of us ever dared to cross him, and here was this…grrrl. She had no reason to want to save me—of all people—and yet she did.

A Mommy's love, she would later call it. Whatever it was, it did what I thought impossible. In that moment, a sliver of my allegiance shifted away from Pan and to Wendi. I knew that this was a heavy burden that I would carry until I could return that favour, maybe longer. It sounds so melodramatic when I say that now, but that's the world we signed up for. Everything and everyone was intense and loaded, ready to explode. Pan played for keeps; dominance and submission was not a game. It was the way of life for all of us.

Stopping Pan had taken all of Wendi's energy, and she crumpled back down onto the shit, trash, and feathers on the floor. Her eyes rolled back in her head. Pan placed his knife back into his belt holster and turned away from me.

I've seen Pan beaten in battle. It isn't pretty, but it only makes him more determined. He is most dangerous when he's under Hook's boot, when he is close to lost. In the days that follow, he will do more push-ups, command more of us bois to wrestle him, and then he will return to Hook to battle again. But now, Pan knelt before Wendi, begging her to live, to awaken. He was bargaining, begging I'm not sure who or what, that if the Wendi Lady were to live, he would be such a good boi for his Mommy. He pledged that we would all be obedient, but she did not wake. He promised that if she woke, she could meet the Mermaids. (I didn't know yet that on their journey to Neverland, he'd promised Wendi femme sisterhood.) Wendi moaned and tossed on the floor, twitching and sweating. It was clear that she was at last beginning to come around, but it was a long way back to shore, and the Crocodile chased, snapping at her heels, as she raced toward Pan. She'd heard nothing of all his promises of servitude, or the love of a boi for his Mommy. All she could see was the shape of his lips, and the raspy, tender sound of his voice.

Wendi was in and out of consciousness. I knew how much she'd taken. There was no way to safely get her into one of our hammocks, so Pan ordered all us bois to give up our softest blankets so he could lay her on them. We each brought Pan the cleanest, softest of our blankets, and he sniffed each pillow to find the ones that smelled the least of hair gel, cum, or B.O. Our Mommy was wrapped in blankets and lay on a patch of floor we quickly scrubbed with the dirtiest T-shirts we could find in the clothing pile.

John Michael sat at the edge of our circle, crouched and leaning against the wall. She was scared, that was clear. When she and Pan had first arrived, she'd asked if Wendi was sleeping. Nibs, more tender than he normally is, responded that she was. This seemed to quiet the boi for a little while, but she became restless, and when John Michael asked why we couldn't wake her and have her cook for us, I glanced at Pan, who was sporting a disturbed and disgusted look in response. Curly was also mortified by this strange boi who so clearly was not one of us. When John Michael suggested that we rouse Wendi, Curly began very slowly to explain, as though John Michael were stupid, that we were building a safe nest for her. No more would Wendi be the group-home sister who would cover for John Michael when she violated curfew. This boi had a lot to learn about how things worked around here.

I guess you could call it consent. After all, John Michael was into Pan, though I'm not sure he really prepared her for what it would mean to be a lost boi. As she helped us to build a nest for Mommy, she looked dazed, as though she couldn't quite figure out what she'd done to get here. John Michael was still thinking about what they had seen in the Jolly Roger. Pan had sneered, but she'd been turned on. The rules, legacy, and boundaries were more enticing now than they had ever seemed when she had read about them in books and blogs. John Michael wondered if Hook's pirates would want a boi like her, not knowing that this thought was pure treason.

As Wendi slept in her nest, Pan fixed coffee on the little two-burner stove. Us bois were sent away, except for John Michael, who was instructed to stay. I took Erebos outside with me. The sky was light and none of us had slept. Time is a strange thing at Neverland. None of us had a watch. Time was about the moment, not what day of the week it was or the hour on a clock. I watched as Erebos pissed in some black-berry bushes at the edge of the train tracks. I felt proud that Pan still trusted me with his dog. Washington, perched on my shoulder, had also gone outside with us. I pulled a marker from my pocket and ripped a page out of a dry newspaper that had blown against the edge of the dumpster.

> *Dear Siren,*
> *It appears that the Wendi will live. Pan had brought her, and she is to be a Mommy to all us bois. I've never had one of those before, but hopefully I'll learn how to serve her, and how to let her care for me. It appears that Pan doesn't intend to kill or banish me, and he doesn't need to know that you were here. I took full responsibility, and so long as she comes to, and I get the hang of this Mommy/boi thing, I think everything will be fine.*
>
> *Pan's lost boi,*
> *Tootles*
> *p.s. I had a really good time with you today*

I let Washington hop onto my fingers, put the note in my mouth, and with my free hand, opened his little leather pouch. Then I folded the note and strapped it in. I kissed the back of Washington's neck and he cooed.

"Take this to the Lagoon, please," I whispered, and his purple-grey body took to the sky, circling me once as he gained speed, then flew over Neverland and toward the river.

When Erebos and I came inside, Pan only nodded his gratitude, but didn't invite me to stay in the kitchen. I went to my hammock. When I climbed in, the damn cock I'd thrown up

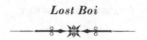
there earlier poked me in the ass. On another day, it would have been funny, but today it just made me angry so I hurled it into the cock pile on the other side of the room. I snarled a laugh, wondering what a Mommy would think of a pack of such filthy bois. I knew enough to realize that wasn't the kind of thing you should let a Lady see. I tried to stay awake, to hear everything Pan said, but when sleep came, it took me hard.

Before I slept, however, I heard Pan trying to bond with John Michael, trying to connect with this boi who'd been to school and conferences, who'd taken 101 workshops, and didn't go out on dates without having every aspect from hand-holding to flogging fully negotiated with kinky checklists completed and compared. She could have joined ranks with Hook's crew, except…there was something about Pan. Maybe she was attracted to his red hair, close to silvering, or his arms encased in thick black tattoos, but I think what drew her were the adventures he promised. I doubt she was naïve enough to believe they wouldn't also come with danger.

I awoke suddenly and steadied myself so as not to fall from my hammock. Around me I could hear the shallow snores of the other bois. I squinted into the darkness and made out three empty hammocks, the two newly prepared ones and Pan's. In the quiet, I could hear someone being flogged in the kitchen.

When a boi joins our ranks, Pan likes to spend private time getting to know them. That new boi time always makes me jealous. I'm poly, so of course I don't mind him being with another boi, but that special first night gets under my skin like a TB test, and I get all itchy and red. I was so riled, thinking about him being with that preppy boi. I didn't have to spend much time with John Michael to realize who she was; it was so obvious that she would never be part of our pack. For fuck's sake, she walked into Neverland wearing a sports jersey. I didn't give a shit if she grew up in foster care, she had snitch written all over her. I don't trust easily. It's a fault, I suppose, except that Pan is usually the same. He never told me to act any different, and he appreciated how protective I was of Neverland; he called me his right-hand boi a couple of times, when the others weren't around. John Michael might have been able to take a good beating, or at least that's how it sounded, but I knew she wouldn't last. I just hoped Pan wouldn't let himself get too attached. He says he doesn't care when bois up and leave, but I know he does.

I forced myself back to sleep, fingering the cuff I'd worn since the moment I became Pan's. It helped to keep me from crawling out of my hammock and wedging myself into the doorway to watch Pan's battle. Normally, he likes an audience to show off for, but for his first time with someone, he likes to give them privacy as they break. Pan likes to give a boi something special to remember him by.

I'll never forget my first battle with Pan. It was terrifying, overwhelming, and confusing, and yet it was also everything I'd ever wanted. Pan was wilder back then. When I first became his boi, he was flying on pixie dust every day. I didn't know what hit me or what I was consenting to when he jumped me in. It was the hardest beating I've ever taken. I wouldn't even call it a true battle, it was so one-sided. I knew I needed to push myself because the stakes were so high. I knew if Pan wasn't impressed, I would be alone again. After that battle, I had to stay inside Neverland for a few days. Between the purple eye and the bruises that lined my arms, thighs, chest, back, and shins ... Well, basically everywhere on my body was bruised. That first night in my hammock, when Pan was done with me, when I knew I had pleased him, when I knew that I was to be his boi, I knew that, for the first time in my life, I was home. It was the best sleep I'd ever had, even though it was impossible to get comfortable with all the cuts and bruises pressed against the ropes of the hammock.

The bois and I awoke to grimy sunlight fighting through the filthy warehouse windows. John Michael was snoring in her hammock, but Pan's was empty. Pan doesn't do mornings. I started sweating and couldn't catch my breath. I was worried that something bad had happened. Waking up alone, not knowing where I am, or not knowing where Pan is, always fills me with the kind of anxiety I can't deep-breathe my way out of. I needed him. Pan was usually pretty good about keeping his nose clean, but pixie dust was so easy to get, and it was always calling to him. It scared me because I knew how much he liked to fly with it. He said the temptation called to him like sweet little bells, not like the gnashing teeth of the Crocodile., and that's how he knew it was safe.

The bois and I rolled out of our hammocks to look for Pan, dragging John Michael with us. We found Pan hunched against the wall under the main window. At first, I worried he'd flown in, but then, when I saw Wendi asleep in her nest, I realized that he was watching over her. Pan would rather die than be a gentleman, but he cared for this grrrl. I'd only ever see Pan save bois, a ritual that's exacting and intense, but not especially tender. He expects those under him to be strong, to be a pack, to hold rank and honour, and to uphold his (messy) protocol. All the jealousy and frustration I'd been holding all night was gone when I saw his sleeping face, its expression both playful and determined. All I wanted was to kneel before him, to make sure that things were right between us. Wendi awoke and asked for more blankets. She must have sobered up but probably felt like shit. Did she act more fucked-up than she actually was? We brought blankets to her because she was to be our Mommy, and I wanted to make her happy. Wendi snuggled back down in the blankets and I made coffee for us all.

When Wendi's eyes opened again later that day, all of us bois dropped to our knees before her. I didn't say anything, but secretly I worried that she wouldn't want us. All us lost bois looked nervous, except for Nibs and John Michael. Nibs couldn't meet Wendi's eyes; he looked instead at the dark, angry line of dried blood on her ankle and scowled. I was afraid that she would get up and climb out the window and leave us before we even had a chance of getting a Mommy. Or worse, that she would remember what I had done and would banish me, deciding to Mommy only the other bois.

What happened next felt like a desperate yet irresistible flirtation between us bois and our new Mommy. Wendi sat up on her makeshift bed and ran her hands through her hair, taming it, as she looked over each of us in turn. There was not a boi who could prevent a deep blush from crawling across their cheeks and down into their shirts. It's not polite to say, but I knew that each of us grew incredibly hard and/or wet, depending on our orientation, under her gaze. We had presented ourselves to her as best we could. I turned to look at Pan and saw that not only was he looking at us approvingly, but he'd also made attempts to comb back his hair and tuck his paint-splattered T-shirt into his sagging pants. Watching him present himself made me queasy. Please don't misunderstand; it's not that I have a problem with switches. My own role in Pan's world is too complicated for that. But to watch Sir present himself to this grrrl was a lot to ask of any of us bois. In fact, it was too much to ask of Nibs, who pulled away from the pack and walked right out the door. Wendi tried to act humble and surprised by the attention we lavished on her. She turned to us bois and Pan, all on our knees. In unison we said, "Oh, Miss Wendi, please be our Mommy, please stay!"

She twirled her hair in the most seductive way, her eyes big and wet. "Oh, I'm just not sure! You bois are so sweet, but being a Mommy is such a lot of work, and I'm only a little grrrl!"

It was only Pan who dared answer; the rest of us held our

breath. "Please Wendi, we'll be good to you. Please stay and tell us stories!"

I didn't want to care, to admit it mattered to me. Us bois had managed just fine without a Mommy for a long time. I wanted to rise and say, "We don't need this pretty grrrl, this wannabe Lady, wannabe grownup," and yet, I'd caught Pan's Mommy fever. Despite myself, I needed this Wendi Lady to be my Mommy, to patch my pockets, to tuck me in. I hated myself for it, but I wanted nothing more than to bring her trinkets, rusted and tarnished bits of jewellery, and to steal bouquets of flowers for her from the cemetery.

Our first unspoken order was that we bois had to work together to convince Wendi to be our Mommy, to stay in our world, and most importantly, keep us as her own. Pan's confidence and pleading made Wendi smile, bat her eyes, and primp up her hair. I don't like to stick my nose in where it doesn't belong, and I didn't really know how Wendi felt about me or the rest of the bois, but it looked like, right away, she wanted something different, something romantic from Pan. She motioned for all of us to get up off our knees. I thought that she was going to issue some kind of a speech, but her words were forgettable. The gist of what she said was that she would stay, be our Mommy. I watched as Wendi kept trying to catch Pan's eye, but he was beaming and looking proudly at us bois.

That first night with her was a special one. Wendi spent the day inspecting Neverland, making note of what was out of place and what she needed to turn it into the kind of place that she could think of as home. John Michael seemed in a daze. She'd had her special time with Pan, and it's none of my business, but I'd guess she forgot all about Wendi while she lay in her little nest sobering up. Now, though, John Michael saw that she truly was just one of us bois, and all the shit she'd done, her good grades and conferences, didn't mean a thing. She seemed like she was in shock. Pan had given her a night, and in the afterglow she followed him around Neverland, trying to please him and get more of his attention, but it was no use. Pan had eyes only for Wendi that night.

Us bois spent the day following Wendi around Neverland. Just as I'd known she would, Wendi turned bright red when she looked into our sleeping room; the pile of cocks was the first thing to go. Pan found them a new home in a few crates. Wendi did all the dishes and filled up half the dumpster with old takeout containers, bottles, and broken things that Wendi felt we shouldn't hold onto. It was a long day as Wendi set us up with different tasks: scrubbing floors, doing dishes, or folding the clothes in the clothing pile. Us bois weren't used to working like that; normally, we were in charge of our own days. The Twins kept whining about having to spend so much time cleaning. Curly told them to shut up and stop complaining. I reminded them that this is what it meant to be good bois for Mommy, and that was what we said we wanted.

In the late afternoon, Wendi said she needed to go out to get supplies for our first family dinner. I worried that she was

just making excuses to chase the Crocodile—I was worried and guilty about having shot her. All us bois watched as she pulled sneakers over her pink chipped toenail polish. The cut on her ankle looked angry, but Wendi was calm and smiling. I turned to Nibs and whispered, "Do you think she's really going to the grocery store?" We mostly ate from free boxes and food pantries that sold dented cans for pennies. The thought of an actual grocery store was so foreign. "She keeps talking about cooking dinner," I continued. "Do you think Wendi really means that? Maybe I should trail her to see if she's going to find Crocodile?"

Nibs laughed. "She wouldn't know how to find her way down to the river. Besides, grrrls like that don't try to drown."

I started to protest that he was wrong, that once the croc gets a taste for blood, it won't let go, and how he should know *that* better than any of us. But Nibs cut me off. "I don't know what that grrrl is up to. Maybe she's going home to her parents. Or maybe she really does want to be a Mommy and play kinky housewife to Pan. I don't know. I don't care. I'm no little, and I don't give a shit what this girl does so long as I don't have to be involved."

There was no fighting with Nibs when he was like this. I left him sulking in the corner, mocking the mirror shine on John Michael's boots and trying to get the Twins to side with him about both Wendi and John Michael.

Wendi walked out of Neverland into the downtown, and I slipped out behind her. She wasn't used to living on the run,

hadn't mastered paranoid focus, and so didn't sense me walking behind her. She hurried along the sidewalk. Next to the grocery store was a flea market, a mix of antiques and trash. The vendors were in a gentrification battle for booth space.

Wendi stopped to look at something on a table, and I hid myself behind a rack of faded dresses someone labelled "vintage." I was pretty sure I had seen them in the thrift store dumpster last week, but now they had sixty-dollar price tags. I could only imagine what Siren would say about that. She'd have been pissed off about the price. I don't make a habit of looking at dresses, and I thought for sure the lady working the booth was going to kick me out, but she didn't.

Wendi was at a booth that looked like a yard sale, with everything from baseball cards and old postcards to toys and shoes. It also had a wide table filled with jewellery and was run by an old man who smiled at Wendi. She fingered a tray of charms, picking through them and putting the ones she wanted into her other hand. I was too far away to see what she had chosen. Wendi paid with a couple of crumpled bills she pulled from her bra. The last of her babysitting money, she would later tell me.

Wendi walked back toward the street but stopped at another booth that sold gourmet doughnuts and fancy buttons and ribbons. The booth was staffed by a straight girl who flipped through a fashion magazine and didn't bother to look up as Wendi helped herself to a spool of light green ribbon. She stuffed it into her hoodie and left the market. I wished that

Nibs had been there to see that Wendi wasn't so innocent. I was beginning to see why Pan had liked her.

Next, Wendi went into the grocery store, and I turned back toward Neverland. I felt bad about spying. Clearly, she really did want to cook for us! I left her there and ran back to Neverland, bursting in and shouting, "Mommy Wendi is making us dinner tonight! We need to finish cleaning everything!" Nibs had gone out, but Curly, the Twins, and I kept cleaning things until Pan came over and said he needed me to go out with him.

We walked quickly toward the Interstate, and he explained that a leather cuff was not the proper way to mark a grrrl, that our Mommy needed something fancier. We stopped at the Pawn Shop and peered in the streaked windows. Pan saw a grrrl he knew who worked there and we walked in, the bells on the door announcing our arrival. He looked carefully at everything in the cases and then spotted it, a birthstone ring, the kind that suburban mothers are given on Mother's Day by husbands who are sent to the mall with toddlers clinging to the seams of their jeans. It had a plain silver band and little gemstones representing each child's birth month. By luck, there were eight cut-glass "stones" on the ring. No wonder some poor mother had had to pawn the thing; she was probably broke, with all those mouths to feed. It made the perfect pervertable gift because, with the addition of John Michael and if you counted Pan, there were eight of us bois whom Wendi would be Mommy to.

"She'd like this wouldn't she?" Pan asked me.

"Oh, yes, Sir! I think Mommy will like it very much," I assured him.

The grrrl working in the shop offered to cut Pan a deal if he'd meet her out back, on her smoke break. Somehow, by the time we joined her in the back, where she sat with a lit cigarette, the ring had been "lost." Pan leaned in with a lighter and a filthy hand to shield her cigarette from the wind, and when the cigarette lit, the ring had slipped into his palm and was quickly pocketed.

On the walk back home, I tried to tell him that not one of us had been born in May as he admired the shining green fake emerald right in the middle. He turned and, with a look that reminded me how inappropriate it was for me to be questioning my Sir, said, "Green is my favourite colour. That stone is for me."

When we got back to Neverland, Wendi was unloading sacks of food into our cupboards. Curly rudely asked how she'd paid for it all, but Wendi just winked. Later, I heard her tell Pan that she'd taken the Darlings' food stamp card when she ran away and maxed it out. Pan had been panicked that they would trace the card, but Wendi said not to worry, and that she'd thrown the card into a dumpster on her way back to Neverland. "Besides, they got that food money to feed me and John Michael, I was only helping myself to what I was entitled to." Pan then laughed and kissed her.

We ate so well that night. Wendi cooked us spaghetti. It

was the best spaghetti that I'd ever tasted. She cooked it in a big pot that I didn't even remember we had. Before the water was boiling enough for the noodles, Wendi let Pan remove the leather cuff from her wrist and tie a lacy mint-green apron tight and naughty around her waist. Wendi poured blood-red sauce over the noodles and served it to us with French bread to mop up the extra sauce. As she did, us bois noticed that around her neck, swinging against her breasts, she wore eight key-shaped charms that hung from eights pieces of mint-green ribbon, which I recognized immediately from the flea market. The top part of the keys were heart-shaped.

"Do you think they're for us?" Slightly whispered.

"I hope not," replied Nibs.

We ate dinner out of chipped coffee cups. Even Nibs, who returned that evening, got one. The little Formica table didn't have enough room for us, so Wendi had us sit in a circle on the floor. She got all excited when she finally served up her own cup of pasta and joined us. Wendi seemed so proud of herself when she gave us permission to begin eating. She explained that this was our first family dinner, and this was how she expected us to eat each night. After dinner, we actually had to do the dishes. Wendi told us that never again would there be stacks of crusted, moldy plates like the ones she'd cleaned that afternoon. Nibs rolled his eyes and Pan stood up, about to punch Nibs right in his disrespectful face, but Wendi reached up and grabbed Pan's arm, shaking her head. I couldn't believe that Pan sat down, that he took orders from Mommy.

Nibs stood up and chucked his cup in the sink. Bits of pasta sauce hit the wall. I thought for sure Pan would go after him then, but he didn't. He obeyed Mommy and continued eating his supper. I wasn't sure how I felt about that. Mommy heaped seconds into our cups.

That was the night she stopped being Pan's fantasy story and became our real Mommy. After the dinner dishes were done, we all sat together. Pan kept wiping his sweaty palms against the knees of his jeans. Finally, he stood and walked to Wendi, then got down on his knees and held out the birthstone ring to her.

"Wendi, this is for you, as a token of our family."

Wendi later told me that she mistook Pan going down on his knees in submission as a marriage proposal. But he did kneel before her, and Wendi covered her face with her hands, tears filling her eyes.

"Oh sweet, sweet boi, "she said. "Yes, of course, I shall take and wear your ring." She held out the fourth finger on her left hand for him to place the ring on. Pan hadn't given any thought to what finger she would wear the ring on; for him, a finger was a finger.

Then, so as not to make the rest of us bois feel left out, she called us to her. We fell to our knees next to Pan. Even Nibs knelt, and I saw a smile cross Pan's face. Wendi untied the eight ribbons from around her neck and said: "Bois, I am so proud to call you mine. I promise to care for you always. A Mommy's heart will always be your home. These are the keys to my heart. You will each wear them, the same way you wear Pan's cuff." She gave the first to Pan, tying the ribbon around his neck, and then moved on to Slightly, Curly, John Michael, and the Twins. When she got to me, I felt my face flush, realizing the magnitude of what I was about to consent to. No longer would I be just Pan's boi; now I would also be Mommy Wendi's. I felt the weight of the charm as she finished knotting the ribbon.

As Wendi stood before Nibs, ready to tie the key around his neck, he looked her in the eyes without speaking, then turned and walked out of Neverland. Pan started to chase after him, but Wendi sighed and tucked the charm into her apron pocket saying, "No, Pan, this is a big change for a boi. My feelings aren't hurt, and a Mommy knows how to be patient. Give him time."

All us bois were fingering the heart-shaped key charms that now hung around our necks, and Wendi turned her attentions to her new ring. She looked at the eight stones: red, purple, white, green, orange, pink, yellow, and light blue. Pan proudly explained that each marked the birthday of one of her bois. "See, this one right here is for Curly, and that green one is for me, of course, and the purple one is Tootles, and the white and orange ones are the Twins." No one dared point out how the Twins' stones should have been the same colour, them being twins and all. Pan said it was true, and so it was. That was the way of Neverland.

Us lost bois, we needed Wendi, which was to be our

greatest weakness. We needed a Mommy; Pan told us so. He needed her too, which made our hunger stronger. We were starving, and finally she came for us. As I've told you, time in Neverland is strange; there is no past for Pan, and as his bois, we too strive to live in the now, so we couldn't remember when he first started to talk about us needing a Mommy, about his desire. He wanted to submit, but more than that, he wanted to be tucked in. And maybe Pan didn't want to lose us. Maybe he saw sharing us with a Mommy as a way to keep us from growing up, as some of his other bois had done. I think, in his own way, Pan knew that he needed more than D/s protocol, more than the high-fantasy-come-true of the life we lived in Neverland, the way of life he has committed himself to always upholding. But Pan couldn't see the future, and he'd never had a mother. He didn't know that even here, where it was all queer and leather, Mommy's job was to grow us up, queer as we were, queer as we would become.

Later, Pan sent me out in search of Nibs to straighten him out. It felt good to still be trusted, to still be the boi Pan turned to when he needed something done. It wasn't hard to find Nibs. He was at the all-night diner, making a cup of coffee last as long as possible. He didn't look surprised when the bells on the door jingled as I walked in. I ordered a cup and sat down, uninvited, at his table.

"Pan wants you home," I said when it was clear he wasn't going to start a conversation.

"Pan does? Or Wendi does?" he replied.

"Does it matter?" I asked.

"Of course it matters! Fuck, I can't believe you're just going along with this! I know you'll do anything for Pan, but—"

"As should you! As we both swore that we would! And not that you should be questioning, but it was Pan who sent me looking for you."

"Lay off it. Fuck, you're the best boi, okay? I'm not trying to compete with you for that, I just was trying to say it's weird, isn't it? All of a sudden, Pan brings home this little grrrl and we're all expected to jump, to obey her orders? That's not what I signed up for, and that's not what I gave my blood for. I'm too old for this shit. I thought Pan was different, I thought I could depend on him, but I can't trust or respect someone who's willing to give away his bois to fulfill some hot fantasy."

At first, I didn't know what to say. I played with a sugar packet, and finally all I could think to respond with was, "You don't mean that. You're just hurt and scared."

Those were fighting words, but Nibs didn't raise a fist, so I continued. "I don't know what's going to happen, but having a Mommy is going to be good. If it wasn't, Pan wouldn't have brought her. When I gave myself to him, I promised to obey without question. Who am I to judge what's good for me? Pan knows best! Besides, she's so good to us—she made us dinner and everything! That's what Mommies do. She's going to take care of us, she's going to tuck us in at night and help us not to be so afraid."

Nibs just stood up from the table and said, "Let's go back to Neverland."

I thought I'd done well, doing what Pan had asked, bringing Nibs back with me, making our pack complete. When we got back to Neverland, Mommy smiled at Nibs but didn't pressure him to take her key. She said it was time for bed. Nibs said he wasn't tired. Wendi sent the rest of us to our hammocks. Then she pulled one of the little chairs into the sleeping area and sat down. We all rolled onto our sides and gave her our full attention as she told us our first bedtime story. It was a sweet tale about a grrrl and a boi and the adventures they have.

One of the things about Pan was that he didn't always do a very good job of explaining things. He didn't think that he needed to. I wouldn't say that I disagreed with him. It takes all the fun away from things when you explain and negotiate everything to death. I've always liked to play hard and edgy, and one of the best things about being Pan's was that he always gave me that. Always. But all that day there was part of me that wondered if he'd take us bois aside and explain how the dynamics would work now that a Mommy was in Neverland. He never did, and that's why I was so nervous when the story ended and she began to visit each of us in our hammocks. Given the nature of our sleeping room, us bois were used to not having much privacy. We knew how to close our eyes, put our headphones in, and go somewhere else.

Mommy came to me and crawled up into my hammock.

I scooted over and adjusted the balance so she could lie next to me. I was the last boi she visited. I think she might have planned it that way. Wendi wasn't as innocent as Siren or I thought when we first saw her. Wendi knew I was Pan's second-in-command. I don't know what Pan told her about me, but maybe she heard that I didn't take well to newcomers, that I didn't trust easily. We lay there together, not talking for a while. The longer we lay next to each other, the more uncomfortable I became. I started getting worried that she might try to talk to me about how I shot her. I could hear her breathing; I'm enough of a predatory switch to know that she was working to quiet her ragged anxiousness. I know how to keep a hammock balanced through just about anything, and I thought about rolling over, kissing her, and taking control of the whole mess. But I felt the cuff on my wrist and couldn't move. First and foremost, I was Pan's boi, and I couldn't disrespect him that way. He'd told me, as was his right as my Sir, that she was to be my Mommy. I needed to follow her lead, to be available to her in whatever way she wanted me.

Finally, Wendi turned to me and ran a warm smooth finger down my jaw and kissed my forehead, and then, cautiously, my lips. I was confused, but returned the kiss. I guessed this was part of what it meant to have a Mommy. I like to think I'm like Pan, that I never ever get scared. Pan let me stay stone. He always honoured that part of how I make sense of myself and my body. It's a known thing, not only between us, but between me and the other bois, and me and Siren too.

Pan could do anything to any of us, but this is one of the few things he doesn't play with, except for when we've asked him to, which I did, once. Anyway, when Wendi started to kiss me, I worried about how to block her touch, how to tell my Mommy that there were things I couldn't give her. I think Pan must have told her more about us than I thought, because she didn't go further and brought her lips back to my forehead before crawling out of my hammock and moving toward Pan's.

My head was heavy with the need for sleep, yet I couldn't stop thinking about everything that had happened, the way that our little Neverland family was expanding and what it might mean for all of us. So completely did I trust Pan then that I was no longer worried about Wendi being our Mommy. I just knew that it would be okay. But as I lay there, I could feel a burning sensation, both at the spot where Wendi's lips had met my forehead and where the cuff gripped my wrist, just like Pan's hand does when he holds me tight.

More than Playing House

It was still dark when I felt someone shaking my shoulder. I could barely make out the tattoo on Nibs' face when I opened my eyes.

"Shhh," he said and motioned for me to follow him.

I climbed out of the hammock, rubbing my eyes, confused. Nibs is tricky because of how old he is. I mean, technically, here in Neverland, age doesn't really matter. As long as you're legal, there's no worry that some scary social workers will chase you down and bust you for squatting. Still, although he hid it beneath blue hair dye, Nibs' age was catching up with him. I could tell that he was probably even older than Pan.

Nibs turned being lost into a career. In the decades since he fell out of his pram, he'd been halfway around the world and back. He liked to brag about all the places he'd been and illustrated his stories by pointing to whatever stick-and-poke ink he acquired in various cities/houses/shows/squats. I don't think bragging is very good form, and I'm not really sure why Pan let him get away with it. Nibs' favourite stories were about his time in Berlin. He spent a few years among all the ex-pats there, making as much art as he could—mostly graffiti-style paintings on boards he would pull out of dumpsters. Nibs had a lover there, a filthy boi who taught him to tattoo and marked his face. I think that boi was as close as Nibs has ever come to settling down. He always got soft when he talked about that boi, but never uttered his name.

They lived in little apartment rooms behind a squatted trans bar. Together, they smoked cigarettes and tagged their bodies and all the walls with intricate abstract designs. In the winter, they huddled together to stay warm when the bar hadn't sold enough beer to buy coal for the little stove they used to heat the apartment. On weekends, they would take a train out of the city to walk around the abandoned amusement park. Nibs always talked about the time he threw ropes and suspended that boi from the frame of the crumpling Ferris wheel. (He shouldn't ever tell John Michael that story; I think it would break her little SSC brain.) I think that boi was the only person he ever really loved, and then he overdosed right there in their bed. Nibs was the one to find him. The way Nibs tells the story, that's when his world ended again. From there, he came back to the States and wandered around for a bit, hopping trains and trying to disappear, until Pan found him.

Nibs and Slightly didn't get along because Slightly was always dreaming of her life before Neverland. For Slightly, it was almost as if being a lost boi was just temporary. It's hard to trust someone who seems like they have an exit plan, who might betray you at any moment. That's what Nibs said he could smell in Wendi too.

"Tootles, I just can't do it. I'm not going to listen to some little grrrl playing Mommy. That ain't my kink, and I refuse to submit to that."

"But we have to; it's what Pan wants! You don't know how it will be. You haven't even given her a chance!"

Nibs pulled out his knife and slipped it between his wrist and the leather. Even though it was the middle of the night and all of Neverland was asleep, I yelled out for Pan. Nibs rolled his eyes. He'd meant what he'd said: once the respect was gone, so was his loyalty. He felt as though Pan had betrayed him, and so he owed Pan nothing.

Pan groggily crawled out of Wendi's blanket bed, confused and frustrated at having been awoken so rudely. His eyes followed to where I was looking at Nibs with the knife in one hand, cuff in the other. The padlock was still intact, but the leather cuff itself had been sliced in half. There was nothing to be said. Pan wasn't one for begging or negotiation. It was over, and he knew it. Pan took the cuff and, without a word, walked back to Wendi's bed.

I started to cry. I didn't want Nibs to go, didn't want him to leave me alone, but I also knew that there was no going back. Nibs' bag was already packed. I reached out to shake his hand, but he pulled me into a hard hug, though normally,

Nibs and I weren't very good about being close to each other, or anyone. Nibs broke away from my embrace and walked out of Neverland, a free boi.

Wendi later told me how, when Pan came back to bed, he was upset but wouldn't talk about it. Instead, he grabbed his knife and pulled her left hand close. He stuck the tip of his knife under the little yellow stone on her birthstone ring and easily pried it loose. The stone went flying across the room into the dust before Wendi could reach for it. "I would have saved that! He might come back." Wendi cried. "Nibs chose to leave, he's gone, and you must forget him," was all Pan said to her before going back to sleep.

The following days were filled with getting to know Wendi and making Neverland the kind of place she felt was decent enough to live in. Wendi and John Michael gave their oaths in blood to Pan and Neverland. We were permitted to watch. I don't know why he waited so long to mark them. Maybe Nibs' departure shook him, or maybe Pan was distracted— that wasn't for me to know. The ritual didn't take long. First, he opened an alcohol swab and ran it across their right shoulders before swabbing the tip of his knife. He took Wendi first. She was a big grrrl, and only a couple of delicious tears ran down her cheeks, but she did not cry out. John Michael, to her credit, also took Pan's blade honourably. When he was done cutting the stars, Pan pulled a black handkerchief from John Michael's pocket and dipped the corners in her blood. "Now you have earned the right to wear this," Pan said,

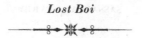
handing it to her. It was a very Hook comment, a very Pirate-like move. Normally, Pan doesn't put much weight in those kinds of rules, but I think he knew it would mean something to a boi like John Michael, and he was trying to connect with her. John Michael put the handkerchief into the right back pocket of her jeans, with the bloody spot proudly showing. Later that night, I caught Wendi in the bathroom twisting to see her oozing shoulder in the little cracked mirror, a smile across her face.

One day, Pan and I went out to the thrift store and, for ten dollars, bought Wendi the biggest couch that we could find. It was velvety and green with a thick, dark wooden frame. It could fit all us bois, or Wendi and three of us. You have to be more delicate when dealing with a Lady; I was working on remembering that. It felt so good to be out with Pan, almost like the old days, and I was honoured to be the boi that he trusted on this adventure to please our Mommy. At first, I was worried about Pan and I both having Wendi for a Mommy, but Pan was still everyone's Sir. He still called all the shots. We didn't talk about Nibs.

I think I started to fall in love with Wendi in those first few days. I'd been so skeptical about her after Nibs walked out. None of us had ever had a Mommy. When we came out as queer and, for most of us, simultaneously as leather bois, we all had gone for Sirs. I shouldn't speak for the other bois, although I know their stories nearly as well as my own. But I can tell you that I played as hard as a Sir would let me, and as deep as I could go. I played for blood and bruises and for scars, the ones you can see and the ones you can't. I wanted to cover up the oldest scars, the ones I got before I was brought out. I (mistakenly) thought then that only masculinity could bring me there. But it was becoming clear that Wendi wasn't skittish, and that she could handle everything us bois laid before her.

Pan could recognize the wildness in our eyes and know how deep and far we'd let him take us in that first battle, but Pan's not one for aftercare. Wendi cared, she cared a lot, and she wanted us to know it. It seemed like all her time was devoted to caring for us. I can only imagine how that adjustment must have been for her, going from being a little grrrl to a Mommy with all these bois for whom she was responsible. At first, it must have been a bit like playing house. I don't mean that as disrespectfully as it sounds either, as playing and make-believe are traits Pan values as much as loyalty. Survival in Neverland is dependent upon make-believe, so in this, Pan and Wendi made a good team. Wendi was blooming in this new world, in this new life. In the early days, she didn't speak about the Darlings or the world she came from. She appeared to be shifting and changing, becoming lost, discovering the way that broken glass sparkles under the glow of streetlights, the way that you can lay hands on another person and watch them come alive under you.

We bois didn't always make the caretaking easy. None of us knew quite what to expect from a Mommy, so the first time

I came back to Neverland with skinned knees after having tried to jump a fence on the waterfront, I thought she would be mad about the rips in my pants. Mommy didn't scold; she looked worried when she first saw me creep in, and the worry didn't pass from her face until she'd felt me all over and was certain there were no broken bones and only a little blood. Mommy took me into our little bathroom, took my pants down, and held me tight while she poured alcohol across my knees. Before Wendi came, the bathroom was filthy, and you would have had to dare me to sit on that floor. With Wendi, the smell of chemical clean came into our lives.

I curled up in her lap, across her frayed pink sundress, the mint-green apron under my head. I don't know what was wrong with me; I'm Pan's boi, I flag black, but here I was, sitting in Wendi's lap, my eyes filled with tears as she kissed away the sting. I'd never noticed before that moment how dark her eyes were. Looking at Wendi, I felt like I was drowning. Unlike Pan, she hated to see me in pain, and having caused me discomfort with the alcohol made her own eyes glisten with unshed tears. I almost came when she put little car-and-wild-animal-print bandages across my scrapes. It was the strangest realization for me that I had no interest in having sex with Wendi, yet I wanted to be with her more than anything. I staggered out of the bathroom, confused about who I had become.

In Neverland, any failure to adhere to the protocol of imagination was punished severely and physically. Slightly, who was a sweet boi, struggled the most with remembering this. She would use scare quotes to talk about a battle, insinuating that it wasn't real, and as I've said, she talked way too much about how sweet her birth family must had been. Her knuckles were always bloody, but she struggled to remember this very simple lesson, one of Pan's most important rules: the world we created and the way that we related to each other was real, more real than anything else, and grownups could never be trusted. I'm proud that Pan never had to beat me for the infraction of forgetting that rule. In some ways, I guess you could say that I'm a simple sort of boi. I wanted Pan and everything about his world that came with him. There wasn't anything worth remembering about where I come from.

I was surprised to see how well Wendi adjusted to our world, not just to being a Mommy to us bois, but to everything about our lives. One morning, right after when she came, she snuck out of Neverland. I first thought that she'd gotten tired of being our Mommy and had decided to leave us, so I started to cry, but she had just gone to the diner around the corner and came back with a Styrofoam cup of coffee. I guess that's part of my trust issues...don't know if that will ever change. Another morning, Wendi left before we awoke but didn't go to the diner. She headed down the tracks to the river and went to the Lagoon. She actually had the guts to walk into the Mermaids' house and try to make friends. It was morning, so they were all home. I suspected that Kelpie felt some type of way about this grrrl, and it would have been within her right to keep Wendi out of the Lagoon, but she didn't. When I asked Siren about it later, she said that Kelpie loved grrrls too much to let any boi get in the way. "Femmes stick together," was one of her mottos. That and "Not gay as in happy, but queer as in fuck you." Kelpie didn't take shit from anyone, especially bois.

Wendi had brought cookies to share with the Mermaids and spent all day with Kelpie. She began to spend a couple days a week with the Mermaids, who fixed her up with some new outfits and taught her how to do her makeup. Soon Wendi traded in all her pink dresses and nail polish for red, "a more appropriate colour for a Mommy of so many bois," she responded when one of the Twins asked about it.

I wondered if Wendi was going to be homesick and drive us all to throw her out of Neverland. I was shocked that she didn't seem to be preoccupied with the life that she'd left behind. It's a thing; when folks have just fallen out of a pram, they often struggle with the adjustment. But Wendi didn't seem worried about anything from her previous life, and for someone who seemed to have everything figured out before Pan found her, that seemed odd. I assumed that she loved us so much that none of that mattered anymore. But I later figured out that she hadn't changed that much. Despite every single fucked-up thing that happened in her short life, it hadn't killed Wendi's ability to trust. Somehow, in spite of every broken promise and crappy system that touched her, she remained confident that all the opportunities she'd built for herself—college, scholarships, everything—would always be there like an open window, waiting for her. I've never met anyone so convinced that things would just work out. I hoped, for her sake, that the world worked the way that Wendi thought it would.

I suspected that Wendi would probably leave us all eventually. That's just the way I am—I expect everyone to leave me. I was just relieved that the Darlings didn't come looking for the children. For the first few days, we were careful to keep the two of them hidden inside. Pan sent me down to check out the stroll where the cops would circle, harassing some of the Mermaids, occasionally ticketing the grownup men. Sometimes they posted missing-persons flyers when they were searching for runaways, but none were for Wendi. I hated talking to the cops, and even though I'd already hit the magic eighteenth birthday, I still flinched when I saw police cars. I don't think you ever really forget how it feels to be hunted. Wendi and John Michael never understood how lucky they were to have escaped out the window without having to live, for years, in hiding.

Wendi turned out to be a tricky one. While she seemed content with her decision to live in Neverland with us, she was also able to hold onto a sense of where she came from: the manners, the education, and her inexplicable trust in grownups. She didn't talk about it with me or any of the bois or even with Kelpie or Undine. Even though Wendi spent a lot of time at the Lagoon, Siren remained aloof from her. It's

not a good feeling to know that you're partially responsible for drowning someone. I should know. It's a dirty truth that Siren and I share, and in a sick way it brought us closer. I am still afraid that one day I'll hear Wendi talk about the Crocodile. Somehow, though, it seems like she's been lucky, and it isn't chasing her.

At first, I really didn't think that John Michael would last a day with us—she was such a preppy baby dyke. I guess our world was more interesting to her than algebra or chemistry classes had been. John Michael might have studied kink in books and tied up a grrrlfriend or two, but that was just baby queer sex. Life at Neverland, on the other hand, was serious, and she had to learn that. I think John Michael was in it to be Pan's, and she was going along with the Mommy/boi thing because it was a package deal, but the hardest thing for her was that she had to listen to Wendi, that she had to call her Mommy.

John Michael did get real close to her pigeon, Bear, and spent most of her time climbing into the rafters to visit with him. And right away, it seemed like John Michael didn't remember much about the life she left behind either. I liked that; it made me feel like maybe I could trust her, at least some day. She started to really understand how if you lived here, if you swore your allegiance, then everything was about Neverland. It didn't take long for her to translate all her reading into practice, and soon John Michael became a battle opponent we could have fun with. In time, we all began to respect John Michael as one of the bois. Everything is about all of us bois together, as a pack.

I guess it began to bother Wendi that John Michael was either forgetting or not caring about the world that they had left, and she started their conversations with remember-whens and don't-forget-hows. I wanted to get up the nerve to ask if it meant Mommy was thinking about leaving, but I didn't have the guts. To ask, to question the realness of our family, would be disrespectful not only to Mommy but to Pan. I couldn't do that.

Wendi liked structure and rules, and she came up with a way to help John Michael remember that there were other choices for her. Wendi insisted that every day after lunch, there would be lessons. I didn't realize it when she started, but she was schooling us on options, on possibilities, on worlds that we had completely removed ourselves from, experiences that Mommy wanted her bois to know about. Had I thought about it that way then, I would have been angry and rebelled, because it was almost like she was schooling us for more than Neverland could give us. I would have rejected that, fought it hard, and I would have confided my suspicions to Pan. If he'd heard it that way, he wouldn't have liked it. Who knows, maybe it would have changed everything. Or maybe he wouldn't have believed me, would have accused me of mutiny and threatened to throw me out of Neverland. Pan's right; second-guessing the past is a fool's game. It's far better to just forget.

After lunch, as I said, we did "lessons." Mommy would ask us to write about the outside. She didn't permit the essays to have anything to do with sex or kink or even queerness most of the time. We had to write about memories of where we came from. I think Pan let her get away with it because, to him, she was still that innocent spoken-word poetry grrrl he had spent months admiring. Mommy had us write our stories, even the ugly stuff that made us punch back tears, and the slivers of broken memories that weren't so ugly. Mostly, I made things up. Neverland was my world. I'd given up everything for it, and I saw no reason to dwell in some little grrrl's fantasy of what could have been. I became most distrustful and disrespectful of Mommy after lunch.

But Curly loved our writing lessons. He always tried to beat John Michael by writing better poems about where he'd been, what he'd done. He wrote about childhood vacations and houses with pretty yards. He was careful not to write about the future, lest Pan think he was making plans. Curly wrote detailed accounts of his life before he was lost, except the details always changed, and John Michael would laugh when the pieces didn't align. I thought it was disgusting, and tried to get out of these exercises whenever I could, but it was a contest, and Pan insisted that not one of his bois back down from a challenge.

We played Wendi's family writing game every day. There was always time for us to write, and then we had to read/perform for Wendi and the rest of the bois. The goal was to slam the best poem based on the prompts and questions that Wendi would give us, like about how we had spent Christmas and other holidays, or what our mothers had looked like. Many of us were just pretending and making things up, but John Michael was a little embarrassed about how much she knew about these grownup fancy worlds. It must have been confusing for her; she knew our world was where she truly belonged, yet Mommy kept pulling up memories of who John Michael had been before and maybe still could be.

When we did our lessons, Pan busied himself with other business. At first, he would stay close to us and play with the pigeons, but after a few days, Wendi asked him to find something else to do, because it riled the birds up and we'd be covered in shit and feathers. Wendi later told me that she thought he didn't participate simply out of spite and hatred for mothers, grownups, and families. This was partly true, but I was the only boi who knew that Pan couldn't read or write very well. He once made me vow I wouldn't ever tell another boi, and most of all that I wouldn't tell Mommy. Pan was so young when he ran away that he'd not had much school. While he could write well enough to send a simple pigeon message, mostly he used me like a service dog to help him navigate a literate world. He probably feared that Mommy, who was so educated, could never have understood. It was an honour for me to be of such service to Pan.

Wendi was trying to tame Pan, that I knew for certain. I first thought she had slipped him something to get him to play along, but he was so committed to pleasing Mommy that he didn't make a fuss when she made us bois sit on little stools and practice polite conversation or walk in neat little lines. When we went out with Wendi, we would come back to Neverland with our clothes clean and not torn; we wouldn't have battles when we were with Mommy. Wendi liked it that way, but I could see it grated on Pan. I think he was more disillusioned with the idea of having a Mommy than he would admit. He wanted to want Wendi, and yet this clearly was not what he thought it would be like. Maybe he was starting to smell the grownup on Wendi; she'd been so close to turning into one right from the start.

He started to go out alone more often. Sometimes I would try to trail him, but he always managed to sneak away. I knew he was going to the Jolly Roger—he'd often tell me about it when he got back to Neverland. Domesticity has never sat well with Pan. It's like trying to keep a dinosaur in an apartment. Every time he came back from his solo outings, I noticed his body was covered with new bruises. It was clear that he was out having adventures and battles with Hook. It seemed to me like the more confused and unhappy he was with having Mommy take over Neverland, the deeper the cuts, the darker the bruises. Wendi would clean and bandage his wounds, but he was bored with her attentions and, words slurring, racing, flying, would create complicated magical stories about being jumped on the street or beaten by the cops, then later he might let slip to me a battle detail. It was not in my nature to doubt Pan, but I've been around a long time, and I know how Pan races on pixie dust. The cuts that lined his shoulders and the boot-shaped bruises on his thighs had Hook written all over them. It confused me that all of a sudden, Pan felt the need to lie. Hook and Pan always battled. They were not lovers and there was no formally negotiated D/s dynamic between them, and yet there was no denying the charge that sparked whenever they were in each other's company. There is a kind of romance that exists between two good-natured enemies, a dance of well-matched battle.

The more Mommy took care of me, the more that she became enmeshed in our world, the less she seemed like the little grrrl who had stumbled in; she became a powerful femme who knew what she wanted. It wasn't that she was more important than Pan, but I began to care very much about what she thought of me. I was angry to see Pan tell her lies, if not explicitly, then implied. Even though Pan was one of us bois, it became clear that Wendi wanted him as a lover. Yet, although she never admitted it, perhaps Wendi knew already that Pan was lost, to her most of all.

Pan loved battling Hook, even if he did laugh at his Old Guard beliefs about good form, rigid identities, and roles. Above all, our Sir was an unapologetic switch, brilliantly able to move within the worlds he built. Pan could be both Sir to us bois and also take a whipping from me or the others—if he was in the mood. He and Hook were evenly matched, and they always left battle covered in sweat and usually blood. As

you know, battle is the word that all us bois used to describe a scene, but never was there a more appropriate word for what happened between Hook and Pan. Ever see two fierce tops go at each other? Nothing is more intense, or hotter. When Hook and Pan were together, it was a battle of mind and will, not simply a show of physical strength. It was as though Pan and Hook were most alive when they were together. They connected in a way that was unlike anything either of them could reach with anyone else.

The leader of the lost bois would always just grin, no matter how hard Hook beat him, no matter how much snot dribbled down Pan's chin as he choked on the Captain's cock. Pan would always pull away, wipe his lips, and make a joke about having enjoyed the codfish. It was infuriating for Hook, the way that boi would never break, would never become his, but there was more to it. They were evenly matched and fought hard for Top. When I watched them battle, it seemed that Hook would become almost peaceful when he was beaten, beneath Pan's gouged and filthy boots. Pan was a good Top, a wise Sir in his own messy way, but even he could never have anticipated what was coming

After Wendi came, Hook and Pan liked it best when they met alone. When there was an audience, they felt like they had to posture and to keep one eye on their bois/crew; neither of them wanted to appear weak. I never got jealous of Pan's time alone with Hook, but I never entirely understood it, either.

Party at the Lagoon

As bois settled into a routine with Wendi. Soon the spring had leapt away, and we were solidly into the hot summer months. Unlike the Jolly Roger, there was no air conditioning at Neverland, and so we bois always spent our summers sticky and irritated, and this often led to fighting that Pan had to break up. We walked around the warehouse in as few clothes as we could stomach. A-shirts and sports bras and worn jeans cut into long shorts became the default dress code. Summer always made me grateful that we weren't Pirates, expected to wear only leather and denim no matter how high the temperatures climbed. For us, summer always brought extra-large helpings of eye candy, with all the bois' muscles bulging and fresh tattoos shown off.

Wendi spent a lot of time at the Lagoon that summer. Siren told me that Wendi had started to relax and spent less time watching her words to ensure they didn't blow the tough-grrrl image she was working on owning. Wendi's dresses had gotten shorter, and instead of the stompy boots the Mermaids preferred when they weren't working, she scoured thrift-store clearance and free boxes for pumps that, in their past lives, had probably belonged to secretaries and saleswomen. I always looked for them too. The first time I bought a pair at the thrift shop, Curly wouldn't stop calling me a cross-dresser and a grrrl. Fighting words. It was fucked-up, but I didn't care to waste the time. I just wanted to get to Mommy. Curly wasn't laughing when we got back to Neverland. Mommy squealed with delight when she put on her new red pumps, and she took me into her arms. My head was right at boob level, now that she wore her new high heels, and Mommy laid my cheek against her chest, kissed the top of my head, and called me her good boi.

Us lost bois spent a lot of time that summer with the Mermaids. Mostly it was lots of fun, but sometimes it was really awkward. One day, Pan found one of Kelpie's necklaces in Neverland and didn't remember who it belonged to, so he gave it to Wendi. That night, when we were at the Lagoon, Kelpie saw her necklace around Wendi's neck and pulled out her little mother-of-pearl-handled knife. Well, Siren put her hand on Kelpie's shoulder, Kelpie put the knife back into her boot, Wendi took the necklace off, and she left it on the kitchen table as we all hurried out the door and back to Neverland.

And while Mommy/boi was intoxicating to me, I didn't

want to lose Siren. One night, I wanted to take her to a show—her favourite riot grrrl band. I ripped one of the posters for the show off a telephone pole, folded it up, and slipped it into Washington's pouch. He came back with a note that said "Pick me up at 7."

It was a sweet night, the kind of night where I, for once, felt like I was doing everything right. I had worked on Pan's boots that afternoon and done the dishes for Mommy before I left. She even sent me out the door with a kiss on the head, her sweet approval of my night out. I arrived at the Lagoon right at seven and handed Siren a rose I'd broken off a bush in some damn yuppie scum's yard. At the show, Siren and I made our way to the front of the crowd. While we waited for the headliner, I pushed her against a speaker. As I ground against her, I could feel her whole body vibrating with the music. After her favourite band finished their set, Siren pulled me past the bar to the grrrl's bathroom and into the back stall. She was wearing a tight green dress and looked so good when I pushed her against the door. She grabbed my suspenders and pulled me to her. After a while, other dykes started to bang on the door, needing to piss. When Siren and I stumbled out together into the now-crowded bathroom, everyone cheered. Laughing but not embarrassed, we made our way out of the venue and onto the sidewalk. I unzipped my hoodie and wrapped it around Siren's shoulders. I didn't have enough money to take her to the diner, so we just kept walking down to the waterfront and up through the dark business district, filled with banks and offices closed for the night and homeless old folks sleeping in doorways.

It was late when I walked Siren back to the Lagoon. She wanted me to stay over, but I knew that Mommy was waiting up for me. Before Wendi came, I used to spend nights tangled in Siren's deep-blue satin sheets, but now I didn't want to. I liked how Mommy would wait up for me, the way she tucked me into my hammock with a kiss on the forehead. So I lied and told Siren that I wasn't allowed to stay out overnight. I don't think that she believed me.

Hook also knew that we had a Mommy, but Pan was always careful to make sure he never met her. Pan liked to keep his worlds separate, and I don't think he wanted to let Hook see him submitting to someone. Sometimes I got jealous of Wendi, but at least I was still Pan's secret-keeper, still his best boi. As always, Pan was reluctant to say too much about his battles with Hook, but one night, as Wendi was reading the other bois a story, he told me that Hook just couldn't let this Mommy/boi business slide. For Hook, everything in life was about demonstrating good form. His most important principle was that, as a top, you could not switch. Even the thought of switching was a breach of honour, the ultimate bad form.

Pan and Hook's battles were gnashing, destructive, yet intoxicating hurricanes. Pan would bottom to Hook in action, but never would he submit. He was his own boi, and that grated on Hook, who wanted nothing more than to destroy Pan, to take him down entirely and leave him begging for his collar. It was no secret what Hook wanted of Pan. He wielded it, somewhere between a threat and a promise, when they battled. Pan only laughed, saying that it couldn't be done, and he challenged Hook to try and make him submit.

Hook never said no to a challenge: another part of his honour. He would carefully remove his leather jacket, leave it hanging off a St. Andrew's Cross in the Jolly Roger's dungeon, and wail on Pan with flogger and fists. Using the hooks labelled with Pan's name, the Captain would send the boi flying into the rafters. Pan would laugh as steel pierced his flesh, and he would lean into the pain, letting the hooks support his weight. Of course, underneath their play was a story, locked in their eyes when they stood dangerously close to one another, Pan's gaze unflinching, and Hook looking down at this boi who would not be his. Despite all Hook's skill and protocol, he couldn't break Pan. Hook's anger spread through him, but Pan could never figure out where it came from. Had he known its root, he would have called it out. That's the way of him. Hook, however, preferred to let things fester, especially things he didn't like. Perhaps, if he'd only been able to set that aside for a moment, things could have looked different, but here I am getting ahead of myself again.

Where was I? Oh yes, the sticky heat of summer. It was the day of the Mermaids' annual play party. When I rolled out of my hammock, I found Erebos panting hard on the concrete floor, with Pan spread out next to her wearing only boxers and a sports bra, talking about the party. Everyone went to it.

Somehow, the grrrls always seemed to pick the hottest day of the year for it, I think because they liked to get everyone as close to naked as possible. All day, Wendi had been anxious, as though this were some sort of family outing, as though our behaviour and appearance would reflect on her as our Mommy. But I'd always loved this Mermaid party, despite the heat, because it was a night full of magic, and I couldn't wait to see Siren again.

The Lagoon's summer party was famous. Kids travelled from a couple of states away to get there, hopping trains and buses or hitchhiking. All the kinky kids did whatever they could to make sure they could be at the Lagoon. It was almost an un-conference of sorts, where if there was something you wanted to learn, someone would probably be up to teach it to you. It was a good place to hone your skills without having to sell your soul and a year's worth of cash to one of the mainstream kink conferences, where we wouldn't be accepted anyway. It was also a place to show off and a great spot to hook up. For this party, the Mermaids sure knew what they were doing. The whole house was decked out with treasures they rescued from free boxes. Kelpie and Undine found strings of green Christmas lights and strung them around the corners of every room and over the doorframes. They wove a web of lights along the widow's walk with its ship's figure-head, a bare-breasted carving of a woman they had attached to the house. The green lights shining against the black trim made the whole house seem dangerous and alluring.

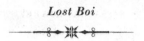

As soon as we got to the Lagoon, we made our formal entrance: Pan first, then Wendi, and then us bois neatly behind them. "Mommy," we asked in unison, "may we please go and play?"

"What do you think, Daddy?" Wendi asked Pan.

I caught sight of Kelpie in the kitchen. She'd clearly heard Wendi, and she was laughing. I mean no disrespect, but it *was* funny to think of anyone calling Pan "Daddy," especially someone who imagined herself his equal. It was a D/s twist of Wendi's own imagination, that together they were Mommy and Daddy over us bois. Pan allowed her this fantasy, I suppose, because of what a good Mommy she was to us, to him most of all. But now he looked so uncomfortable at the word "Daddy" directed at him, and the question seemed to hang in the humid air. He blushed uncomfortably before twisting his face into a bemused smile. Then he nodded to us bois, and we rushed off to explore the Lagoon and see who had washed into town.

I went straight for the widow's walk. The chance to battle outside is one of my favourite things about the annual event. It's another world: there you are on this little strip of deck above the filthy churning water, and it's just you, your opponent, and the stars. Those brilliant stars watch over us, laughing, mocking, maybe smiling, but unable to act on their own. Probably the closest to religion I ever got was up on that roof, lost in a battle. I wasn't quite sure who I'd battle that night, and honestly I wasn't sure I cared. I was out for blood, mine or someone else's.

Everyone was scoping each other out. I had my eye on a boi from Denver, but he disappeared into a bedroom on the top floor of the house with Curly and Undine. I wasn't in the mood for big scenes with crocodiles, and besides, I didn't want to abandon my view of the stars. I imagined myself a wild animal lying in wait, knowing the right thing would come my way: either prey or an even bigger predator. I lit a cigarette and sat on the rough decking, staring up at the stars and picking at the peeling black paint. I'd dressed carefully for the party: black A-shirt, ace bandage for extra flatness, dark denim, and of course, my boots. I hoped my slouching posture was sexy and didn't make me look like I was pouting.

I sat in this same spot last year, and it was Pan who came for me. Sitting here again made me wonder if he remembered that night. When Pan and I battled, I felt cracked open. Our battles were the source of all the magic of who we were. Last year at this party, I was sitting on the balcony, staring off into the black water, when he appeared. Pan can do that, just pop up out of nowhere. Anyway, there he was, standing there, waiting for me to feel the burn of his eyes on me.

"Boi," he whispered, "do you want to fly?"

I thought for a moment that he was talking about pixie dust, and I'm not saying I haven't tried it, but ... I try to stay away. Then I saw the rope coiled in his hands.

Pan has never been one for fancy play. He likes his fists best of all and has been known to make quick use of his belt when the mood strikes him. I'd never seen him with rope before.

"Well?" He was grinning, waiting for me to take my eyes from the rope. The way his small hands were tangled within it, I could just make out the B, O, I, and S of his "LOST BOIS" knuckle tattoos.

"Yes, Sir." I lifted my gaze to meet his green stare. And then the ropes flew. I don't know where he learned to tie sailor's knots, but I found myself bound and secured and hoisted up off my feet, the rope held tight by the eaves of the Lagoon. Suddenly, it was just me and Pan, alone except for the millions of stars watching, laughing, witnessing. The pain of the ropes against my muscles fell away and I was soaring without fear, trusting implicitly that Pan had me, that the magic we created was bigger than us both, that it could hold us. I'd never doubted my place as Pan's boi, but nights like that took me farther than I had ever been.

This year, it wasn't Pan who came to me, it was Wendi. Suddenly, I wanted nothing more than to show her the stars; I wanted to flip her body into the night sky. I've always been a switchy boi, but I think this was the first moment when I really understood wanting to top, wanting to create a world for someone, even for an hour or two. She was standing before me, and there was no time to think deep thoughts about identity or regret, or about not having paid attention when that rope rigger from SF was staying at Neverland. I threw my cigarette into the river and closed my eyes as Wendi ran the chipped red edge of her nail along the line of my jaw and then down my throat, stopping at the ribbed collar of my tank top. It wasn't what I expected.

"Sweet boi, my sweet boi," she whispered in my ear before kissing me. I felt her creamy lipstick smudge against my lips as I wrapped my arms around her. "Mommy…" I moaned as I dug my dirty hands into her dress and nuzzled against her breasts. I thought she was going to beat me, to punish me for not having finished the dishes before we left Neverland like I had been asked to, but I guess she'd forgotten, or didn't care. Mommy wasn't after blood and tears that night. I didn't know what else I could possibly offer to her.

Wendi stood over me. I was confused and torn as I slouched against the railing, legs spread before me. In part, I felt that I should be trying for sexy, to maintain some aloof, tough-guy image. I moved my left hand just slightly, to rest on my thigh. I was hard packing tonight, just in case. I thought maybe Wendi was looking to get laid, to lose herself for a little bit in something that felt completely good, to give herself the chance to forget how messy her life had become. I was just about to lift my hand to rub my stiff, denim bulge. Wendi stood reapplying red lipstick in the soft twinkling light. She stared into her pretty silver compact before closing it with a snap and tucking it into the front pocket of her apron, then she crouched, breasts only inches from my face. All I could smell was the sweetness of her soap, and then she whispered in my ear.

"Sweet little boi, what are you doing out here by yourself?

Mommy has been so worried. She's been looking for you everywhere." I shivered and a smile crossed her face. "Come here, sweet boi, Mommy has something to teach you..."

I'd never wanted anyone in the way that I wanted Mommy in that moment. I watched as she quietly closed the door to the deck, and we were truly alone. She sat next to me, pulling me against her. My cheek rested on her right breast. She was so warm. I closed my eyes. One arm was around me, holding me tightly to her, the other... I'd rather not say, except I must. She was exploring all the places I keep covered, all the places I'd rather forget about, the places I don't even touch, and then she was in them, and I needed more of her, wanted her to take everything. I didn't go away, didn't close my eyes and drift away. I stayed with her, my eyes fixed on the twinkling stars. I hoped they weren't laughing at me. I gave Mommy everything, even something Pan didn't have.

I didn't know until she was holding me, our sweat-slick bodies sticking to the splintered deck, that she had watched as Pan disappeared into a room with the Twins. I wasn't close to them, and neither was Pan, so I was surprised that he chose them to battle that night. They were the most recent arrivals at Neverland before Wendi and John Michael. Their bright mohawks stained the sink and the ropes of their hammocks. The Twins met as teenagers in some backwards town where they lived at opposite sides of the trailer park but were always sneaking into each other's bedroom windows. The minute they turned sixteen, they were gone. I know that they hopped trains and lived in the wilderness together, doing some kind of crazy off-the-grid backpacking for months somewhere between San Francisco and Seattle. When I talk about them that way, it makes it sound like they're urban primitives, which they totally aren't; they're tough, rugged punks who know how to survive outside, but they don't get all fucked-up and appropriative about it, acting like it's some ancient spiritual thing from some tribe, some people they have no connection to. The Twins just like nature and shit, I think, so they hit the backwoods trails. After that, they train-hopped down to New Orleans and all through the south. They play hard; I guess that's probably why Pan chose to spend the party with them. Their backs are covered with scars, interlocking designs left by the steel of knives. None of us ever asked to borrow their binders because they were always crusted with blood from healing cuts. The Twins always liked to irritate the cuts and disrupt the healing. They played for scars.

Wendi and I were still lying together on the deck when the quiet of our breathing was ripped apart by the growl of a bike motor. Pirates. Sticky and trembling, the last thing I wanted was to move, to leave Mommy, but I knew my service to Pan still had to come above all else. I couldn't meet Wendi's eyes as I stood and pulled my jeans over my boots and cinched my belt. I didn't bother with my unused cock and harness, and pulled my shirt on as I opened the door and went into the Lagoon.

I stood silently in the doorway, my fingers picking at the

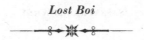
carved initials in the doorframe. Pan had the Twins secured to bolts in the moulding. He sensed me standing there and turned with a look of concern. I was his best boi; he knew I wouldn't interrupt unless it was important.

"Pirates," was all I needed to say to set him in motion. Pan snapped off his latex gloves and threw them to the floor.

"Tootles, see to the Twins." He hurried from the room. I let the Twins down from the wall. If I hadn't been feeling so sorry for myself, so torn, I probably would have been sweeter to them. Instead, I mumbled something about seeing their shirts in the corner. I wanted to be a good big... not quite brother, but something like that for them, but I just couldn't bring myself to give them the aftercare I was lacking. I followed Pan into the living room where Siren, naked except for her boots, torn fishnets, and a tangled net of pearls, reclined on a chaise longue, smoking through a vintage cigarette holder. There was no denying her glamour as she welcomed Hook and his crew to the party.

I knew without needing to be told that Pan wanted me to disappear into the shadows and hide Wendi. She was still the kind of grrrl who could easily be misled or seduced by ritual and rules, the kind Hook loved and which bored Pan immensely. This was part of why he hadn't allowed Wendi and Hook to meet; he knew she would love the Pirate's good form. Pan kept her from the Pirate Cove, a BDSM club downtown, too. The Cove was never really our scene, but sometimes, before Wendi joined us, we would go there and battle. Mostly though, we just watched the parade of sashes and laughed at these people, for whom it was a performance and not a lifestyle.

The mood of the party shifted with the arrival of the Pirates, who couldn't be missed in their pressed and starched Levi's, black T-shirts tightly tucked in, black leather belts, boots, and vests. Smee and Hook wore leather chaps, and Hook the cap and jacket that marked him as their leader. They carried play bags with exotic wood carved into oar-shaped paddles, beautifully braided floggers, and single tails.

Before I slipped away to hide Wendi, I saw Hook and Pan greet. Watching them was always like watching a thunder-storm—you could feel the electricity in the air and knew you couldn't get too close because you would get burned. Hook and Pan exchanged nods. For all the rivalry, there was a pro-found respect between them. They shook hands too; Pan's filthy little tattooed one disappearing into Hook's strong leather-clad grip. They always stared deeply into each other's eyes when they met, not daring to drop their gaze. Although Pan respected his bois, as our Sir he wouldn't have wanted to be seen by Hook as one of us. I don't really know how Hook saw things. He needed his crew; after all, what's a Master without someone to serve him? In that way, I think his crew was valuable to him, especially Smee (who I think was more lover than boy). Hook valued his crew, but I don't think that he respected them. He didn't respect anyone who wasn't a lifestyle Top.

I couldn't get to Wendi in time. She was coming down the stairs as I pulled my eyes away from the Pan/Hook storm brewing in the living room where Siren watched too, blowing smoke rings at them. Wendi was all stockings and pumps. The first several buttons of her dress were undone, bra showing her flushed chest. It was clear then that she was already turning, that womanhood would take her. Still, I didn't want to believe that she would leave, betraying us all, becoming a grownup. I didn't want to think about the choices I would have to make, what I would want.

"Daddy, don't you think we ought to find the littles?" Wendi asked. Her sweet voice suddenly turned hard. I saw Pan flush, his little fists balled at his sides. This Daddy thing was purely Wendi's fantasy. Again, I mean no disrespect to my Sir, but Pan was no Daddy. Hook, whose good form wouldn't permit a ruder response, cocked one eyebrow at Pan and smirked.

"Been experimenting with new roles?" he whispered. "What's that cute girly key around your neck?"

Pan's face quickly switched from embarrassment to anger as he turned, and he said nothing as he grabbed Wendi's hand and went deeper into the Lagoon.

I thought we might leave the party then, but we stayed on. Pan and Wendi had slipped into a little room under the stairs, and I was left alone. I thought about finding a Pirate to battle with, but I wasn't in the mood for blood or sex anymore. More than anything, I wanted to be left alone to think, to try to make sense of everything that was happening. I sat on the stairs, feeling like our old globe when I spin it really fast, so fast that you can't tell what cities or countries are whirring past you, so fast you can't tell who anyone is, or where they are from. I didn't know who I was anymore, what I was doing, or where I was from. All I wanted to do was spin the globe faster so that it would never stop, so that I would never have to remember, never not be dizzy, never have to figure out where I was going.

After a few moments, Pan reappeared and brought one of his dirty fingers up to his lips to signal that I should remain quiet. I didn't try to follow him. I wasn't sure that I was really up for any kind of adventure.

He went into the bathroom and closed the door. Pan knew how the heating vent in the bathroom connected, through the ducting, to the big bedroom by the front door, the room the Pirate crew always commandeered when they came to battle. Standing on the toilet, Pan listened through the vent to the sounds of slaps and moans. It was a messy ruckus, which meant only one thing: Hook wasn't in the room. Pan must have seen that Hook had stayed in the living room, talking at Siren about some new toy or conference he had been to. Hook was always trying to impress her, but Siren couldn't have cared less. She liked to fuck and could get into BDSM when the mood struck, but she found D/s boring. I'd tried to explain to her why I needed to be Pan's lost boi and what having a Mommy meant to me, but it just didn't make sense to her. Siren wanted a boifriend.

Pan hunched over and giggled before straightening up and tucking his thumbs into his belt loops. Standing on the toilet, he puffed up his chest and bellowed "Crew!" directly into the vent. The slapping and moans were replaced with scuffling and then a tentative "Yes, Captain?" in unison.

Pan had to double over in giggles again, his boots braced on the piss-slick seat. This was going to be one of his best pranks ever. Pan knew Hook better than anyone, except for maybe Smee. You always know your lovers different than you know a battle opponent, but Pan had spent years learning Hook's manners and style, and he did a pretty mean imitation of his voice, especially when distorted through an air vent. Hook's crew was completely fooled.

"Release those grrrls!" Pan commanded in Hook's voice. He couldn't see them, of course, but heard the confused whispers about why the Captain would have brought them to a party only to take away their fun just when it was getting good.

"Maybe it's a test?" suggested one of the Pirates.

"Maybe…" Smee started to say, then shook his head in confusion. *No*, he reminded himself, this was not confusing. The Captain had given orders, and they were to be followed. There was nothing simpler.

"You heard the Captain," shouted Smee. "Release the grrrls. What are you, a bunch of lost bois without proper form? It's a good thing Captain Hook isn't standing here to watch you disobey him. Think of how you would be punished if he saw. Hurry, or I'll have to tell him."

Pan climbed off the toilet and walked into the hallway, seeing the grrrls—mostly femmes he didn't know—quickly leave the room, straightening corsets and reapplying lipstick, then walk into the living room or out the front door to smoke on the porch couch.

Hook was deep in conversation with Siren, asking about us, about Pan, about how we had found a Mommy, and how it seemed like everything was changing. Pan and I both saw that Wendi had now come out from under the stairs and was listening to Hook. She was pleased that the conversation was about her, about how important she was to our lives, and how she was helping us to dream of something different.

Confusion crossed Hook's face at the sight of his crew standing before him. Pan was now laughing so hard, I worried he was going to piss himself. He tried to muffle his laughter, so that Hook and the Pirates wouldn't catch on. Hook looked at his blueballed crew, then at Pan, then back at the crew, trying to make sense of what was happening. Then his eyes locked on Pan, and what I saw seemed like admiration. Pan had controlled his laughter and met Hook's stare as Wendi crossed the room and introduced herself to Hook as our Mommy. He took her hand and gently kissed it.

Smee broke the silence and asked Hook what a Mommy was. Wendi gasped. For a boi to not know the love of a Mommy shook her deeply. Perhaps that was her greatest similarity to Pan: since coming to Neverland, she had lived this fantasy entirely. No, let me correct myself. That is how others, outsiders, might see this, but for her, for us, none of this was a fantasy. There was no role that Wendi took more seriously than being our Mommy. We were her bois, and when Mommy heard Smee, there was a piece of her heart that broke for him, even though he was a Pirate in a proper Leather uniform. I think in that moment, there was a part of her that wanted him as her own.

Pirate Jukes then suggested, quite out of turn, that they should kidnap Wendi and force her to be their Mommy. My hands became fists, but I saw from the corner of my eye a look from Pan, the kind of look that was really an order, and the kind of order I knew better than to disregard. This was a test for Wendi, who, at the thought of being taken from her bois, us lost bois, shouted, "*Never!*"

There was nothing else to say. Pan grinned and nodded first to Hook, then to me, before walking back down the hallway. He knew that Hook wouldn't want to take a grrrl against her will, that consent was too important to Hook's code of honour. Pan knew that his Mommy would be safe for as long as he wanted her, or for as long as she would have us.

Hook dismissed his crew and they, confused and slightly irritated, went back into the front bedroom, calling out the window to the grrrls smoking on the porch that they should come back in and battle. Not long after, Pan heard the commotion start again. He went into the bathroom again and locked the door, climbed onto the toilet seat, and listened.

Soon all he could hear through the vent were moans and the sound of leather and flesh meeting.

It was too easy, but he couldn't resist. Again, in his best Hook voice, Pan called into the vent: "Why do you keep me waiting? Release the grrrls and present yourselves!"

Pan now heard a different sort of moan and confused wailing, and then the sounds of flies zipping and boots angrily marching out of the room. This time, he stayed in the bathroom and waited. Hook marched his crew back into the front bedroom to scold them in private. Pan could clearly hear Hook's lecture about how foolish the crew was, how clearly he hadn't given them orders, twice, to end their battles. He dismissed them again. Pan knew the sound of Hook's boots and through the vent heard the Captain's heavy steps on the old hardwood floors. Pan knew he was caught, which only made the adventure of it all the sweeter.

"Who is giving false commands to my crew of Pirates?" Hook yelled into the empty bedroom.

"It is I, Hook, Captain of the Jolly Roger!" Pan responded in his best imitation of Hook.

"If you are Hook, then who am I?" Hook called out, his voice sharp with irritation.

"A codpiece."

Pan knew that he was playing dangerously, pushing things a little too far, to insult Hook this way. For a moment, Pan felt bad about it, imagining what it would be like to be humiliated in front of his lost bois, but then he forgot this dark thought, as he forgot most of them. After all, Pan knew that he was far too clever to be tricked like this.

"Reveal yourself, insolent boy!" Hook knew he would reel Pan in, punish him, and remove whatever shame might have tarnished him in the eyes of his crew. Pan unlatched the bathroom door and stood in the doorway, grinning until he felt Hook's eyes peering around the bedroom doorway and down the hallway.

They would have battled, I'm sure. I was sitting in the living room, watching Pan lean against the bathroom doorjamb and rock back onto the heels of his boots. He was ready, cocky, and proud of himself. Pan was never happier, never hotter, never harder than when causing mischief. Then the back door of the Lagoon opened and in walked the Crocodile.

Gator hadn't been invited, but she figured at least one of the Mermaids or their guests would feel like drowning. She looked hot, as always, dressed in a skin-tight black dress, her green hair hanging in a messy tangled braid down her back. It swayed from side to side as she walked, like a tail. Gator was so skinny that if I didn't hate her so much, I'd have tried to fatten her up with pasta and dumpstered bread. All Gator cared about was that her bra was lined with green bills when she walked back out the door.

It took a lot to pull Hook's attention off Pan, but the Crocodile always could. Hook started to sweat and shake. The Crocodile had its hold on him. Pan didn't even need to turn around to know Gator had arrived. Pan signalled to me. For us, the party was over. There would be no more battles that night. I led Wendi and the bois back to Neverland. When we got home, I expected to find Pan in the rafters with the pigeons, but he wasn't. Wendi didn't understand the hold the Crocodile had on Hook or why this mattered so much to Pan. The next day, Siren told me that Pan had stayed near the Lagoon. He waited for Hook, standing outside and leaning against Hook's chromed motorcycle. Pan later told Siren that he'd considered making a deal with Gator and throwing all her baggies of Crocodile at Hook's feet to make him choose once and for all what was most important, to see if Hook was strong enough to turn it down. Hook talked such a big game about good form, but Pan knew Hook was just barely out-swimming the Crocodile, that every so often, it would drag him under. Pan wanted Hook more, in that moment, than he had ever wanted the Pirate.

The Apology

hen Pan saw Gator leave the Lagoon, he went back to the house, passing Kelpie and Siren, who were on the porch couch smoking with some femmes from New Orleans. Pan nodded at the group and began to search for Hook, whose crew was hanging out in the living room. Smee looked up when Pan came in, but gave no clue as to where his Captain was. Pan searched through all the basement and first-floor rooms, where folks were drowning and fucking and making out. When he went upstairs, he saw that the door to the widow's walk was ajar. Hook didn't need to turn around when Pan came outside; he recognized the sound of the boi's boots against the rotten decking. Hook stared up at the stars. He was not drowning. Pan stood next to him, trying to get Hook to look at him, but Hook wouldn't acknowledge him. Pan sighed. "You aren't still pissed about earlier, are you?" Pan asked, playfully grabbing one of the Captain's belt loops. "You know I think of you as more than your codpiece." Hook refused to respond. "Oh, come on, Hook! Don't be mad at me! I was just messing around, I didn't mean any harm by it. Can't we just let it go? Let's start this night over."

Finally, Hook—still looking at the sky—said, "You owe me nothing short of a formal apology for the way you acted tonight."

Pan did not roll his eyes. He straightened his shirt the way Mommy had taught him, wiped his grimy hands on the back of his jeans and, when he was convinced his hands were clean, extended his right one toward Hook.

"Captain Hook, please accept my apology. I acted out of turn this evening, disrespecting you in front of your crew. I let my joking go too far. I am truly sorry, and I am here to ask for your forgiveness."

Hook pulled his eyes away from the stars and turned toward Pan. "Look at you. Little boi, if I didn't know better, I'd say you were a grownup standing before me. I hear that you're a Daddy now. Looks like that grrrl figured out how to make a man of you, and you like it, don't you? You like being her husband? Being a grownup?" And then Hook spat right on Pan's outstretched hand.

Pan winced. They were fierce battle opponents, but Hook had never been cruel to him before. Closing his eyes for a moment, Pan took a deep breath, wiped Hook's spit off on the back of his jeans, and smiled. Pan is different from all us other bois in that he doesn't hold onto the hurtful, unfair

things in the world. Just as a boi who grows up and leaves Neverland is immediately forgotten by Pan, so are hurts. Pan smiled at Hook, and again extended his hand.

Hook was disgusted—with himself and with Pan. This filthy boi, leader of a gang of hoodlums, had exhibited better form than he had, the Captain whose workshops on protocol people paid money to attend. More to the stars than to Pan, Hook angrily asked, "Aren't you ever bad? Doesn't your form ever falter?" Without waiting for Pan to respond, Hook turned and walked back into the Lagoon.

Pan was left alone with the stars. He was confused, but had already forgotten the hurtful sting of Hook's words. Tink came to him, accompanied by a whole flock of Neverland's pigeons. They perched on the railing and on Pan, tickling him with their dinosaur feet and flapping wings until he laughed and completely forgot all of it.

The Unhappy Home

It was a time of coming together, of truly being a family. Wendi threw herself completely into her role as our Mommy. She also reinforced old power hierarchies, often telling us to "listen to your Daddy." Of course, that was just business as usual for me and the lost bois. I never thought of disobeying him. I took my commitment extremely seriously and distrusted those who didn't. No one could say I didn't give Pan the best of myself.

For a time, it seemed that John Michael had fallen in love with the Neverland magic. I know I wasn't very fair to her at first, but by now she had truly become one of us lost bois. It would have been dishonourable for me to doubt her loyalty. She'd stopped her lectures about what was the "proper," or "safe," or "appropriate" way to suspend or punch someone and yet, although she was one of us, she seemed happiest when battling with the Pirate crew. Sometimes I wondered if Pan regretted bringing Wendi and John Michael to Neverland—but here I am thinking like a grownup. The best thing about Pan was that there were no regrets. He lived perfectly in the moment, without doubt or questions, trusting completely, and when Wendi agreed to be our Mommy, he gave us bois to her. I think that he believed that because she was a Mommy she could get John Michael under control. John Michael never respected Wendi as a Mommy, and she certainly didn't respect Pan, not outside of battle, where it mattered the most.

When Pan would go out, John Michael would talk to Mommy in a disrespectful tone. She would ask to sit in Pan's spot or to play with his knives. There was always battling among us bois, much of it good-natured fight-picking, but this was different. It seemed…toxic. Wendi didn't know how to handle this boi she had known as a brother, but here had negotiated to care for as a boi.

Pan became increasingly preoccupied by Hook and therefore spent less time with me. I responded by acting out to get Pan's attention—not anything big, just simple things. Pan would say:

"Tootles, black my boots."

And I would respond, "Okay."

I had been trained better than that. I knew the protocol, and that only correct response was, "Yes, Sir!"

I'm not proud to admit it, but a slap across the face felt better than being ignored. The further away he felt, the more I was almost afraid that I would lose him. In those moments,

I latched onto Mommy's apron strings, and I wasn't sure if I cared where Sir went, with his pixie dust and Pirate battles. I was angry that he didn't take care of John Michael, that he didn't get rid of her, if that's what it would take, like he'd done before with other bois who hadn't worked out. Worst of all, I started to doubt him.

One time, Pan and I came into Neverland to see one of the Twins doubled over on the floor. He was turning blue and mumbling something about train tracks.

"What the hell happened here?" Pan asked the other Twin.

He didn't respond right away, so Pan threw him against the concrete wall, forearm across his throat. He sputtered and tried to talk, and Pan pulled his forearm away a little. The Twin confessed that they had been down by the river chasing the Crocodile, and maybe they had dived too deep. I knelt over the first Twin. It was obvious what was happening, his pupils were so small, and when his skin started to turn as blue as his hair, I got up and yelled at Pan who still had the second Twin pinned against the wall.

"Give me quarters! Please, Sir!" I tried to soften my demand to a respectful request, but my tone was all wrong.

Pan turned. He knew why I wanted the coins, knew that I intended to run to the corner payphone and call for an ambulance.

"No one is going anywhere," Pan responded, stepping away from the second Twin who slumped to the floor and turned his attention to the first Twin.

"Bring me my bag. Now!" he ordered me.

My hands shaking, I brought Pan his backpack. From the front pouch, he pulled out the Naloxone, which harm-reduction street-outreach teams had just started to hand out and train kids how to use. Pan roughly tilted the Twin's head back and sprayed the anti-overdose drug up his nose. Time in Neverland seemed to stop, but within a minute the Twin's breathing deepened, and the only thing blue about him was his Mohawk.

That night, Pan ignored the Twins as they comforted each other through withdrawals. Wendi was having a slumber party at the Mermaid Lagoon and so wasn't home to hear the Twins call for Pan. I could make out their whispered cries, saying they couldn't take the pain, and they wanted to detox in the hospital. I reached for my boots, preparing to go outside and call a cab. I'd stolen quarters out of John Michael's jeans earlier in the evening, just in case, so I wouldn't have to ask Pan again.

"If you go to the hospital tonight, you are no longer my bois," Pan replied. "You aren't overdosing anymore. You feel like shit, and you should. You will be sick, and maybe you'll think differently before chasing the Crocodile again," Pan said coldly from his hammock.

I went to Pan, but before I could say anything he gave me a look. "Surely you aren't doubting me, are you, boi?" he said. I went back to bed. Besides battling harder than anyone else, what bonded us was our love of these bois, our belief

that Neverland was the way to save lost and broken kidz, to keep them not only alive but safe and protected. That night, I started to lose respect for Pan. It wasn't something we could talk about.

I started to fight a lot with John Michael. I wanted to break her face. John Michael's lack of respect for Pan, perhaps because it reflected my own unexpressed feelings, brought me to quick anger. Just the sight of her made me feel worse than dope-sick. I kept trying to initiate battle, thinking that might take the edge off. I'm the kind of boi who breaks all the con-ference rules and plays mad. She isn't that kind of boi. She turned me down and asked me if I had something I needed to process. That only made me angrier.

It wasn't against the rules to be angry like that, to want someone's blood. We'd all pledged blood, but we weren't per-mitted to keep secrets. I was supposed to talk to Pan. My rage was the first real secret I kept from him. I didn't even know why I did it, maybe because I didn't want to tell him that the magic was slipping away. It's not like I went out and started planning insubordination; it just happened. Wendi knew, even though I didn't tell her. "Mommy always knows," she would whisper as she tucked me in. She didn't tell Pan either, and so it became our first secret.

Neverland began to feel small. From the moment I'd arrived, I'd been like Pan, never wanting anything else, never lusting for a different life. Other bois did, and that's why they left. It wasn't sudden; I think I would have noticed if I had come home and suddenly seen our world through another's eyes. I could have taken that to Pan, I could have asked for his help, but my questions and dissatisfaction rolled in slowly, like a fog, and once I was surrounded, I couldn't see his magic. All of Neverland had changed, or maybe it was me who changed.

What had once been mystery and adventure now felt like a burden. I saw the empty cupboards, felt the knotted rope in my stomach when there hadn't been enough food to free-box, when Mommy stood and stirred an empty pot and heaped imaginary pasta into our chipped cups. One night it rained so hard that the pigeons' nests and our hammocks flooded, so we all roosted together on the kitchen floor. Once this would have been an adventure, but now I just felt wet and cold. It was only Pan who found magic in the scabies we got from the Mermaids and the bed bugs that came from the mattress abandoned by the Urban Primitives that we carried into Neverland for Mommy. It looked really nice with the heavy, metal police barricade we snagged after the Pride parade to use as her headboard. The whole setup was great for bondage, if you didn't mind the bugs in the mattress. I loved being Pan's lost boi, but I couldn't stop thinking of all the kids even more lost than me and how I couldn't help them. Pan didn't know that my ability to believe was faltering; I just couldn't reach him. No, let me not dishonour Sir. The truth was, I didn't want to reach Pan any more. I let our world, the one he and I built, the one in which his belief never wavered, slowly slip away.

Mommy had taken to calling Pan "Daddy" all the time. I hadn't ever had a Daddy, so I was no expert, but I knew that to be a Daddy, you had to be a grownup, Pan's greatest sworn enemies. He was my Sir, captain of adventure and danger, who left us bloody, glassy-eyed, and on our bruised knees, begging him for more, asking him to turn us inside out, fling us through his slingshot. Anything that he wished was all that we wanted. Mommy thought it was disrespectful that we didn't play family the way she did, but I didn't want no fucking Daddy.

One afternoon, us bois had been wrestling and battling all through the kitchen, and just generally being nuisances. Wendi told us to go outside so "Mommy and Daddy could have some grownup time." The words slipped like silk from her mouth. I don't think she even realized what she'd said. Pan was in the rafters and couldn't hear, which is all that kept his fist from her cheek. John Michael had a Twin in a head-lock, and Curly looked like he was trying to sneak into the bedroom with the other Twin, whose hand had slipped past the loose waistband of his jeans when Mommy's order came down. I was the only one who heard her slip. I flashed anger then worry, but kept it off my face.

I made the decision right then to disobey her, and I sneaked back in as the bois hit the street, half going to spange coins outside the diner and the others to the Lagoon to see if any of the Mermaids were home. Alone, I climbed onto the dumpster behind Neverland and peered in through a sooty window cracked with BB holes. I lay on the dumpster with my head just below the window. I knew that Pan and Wendi, curled together on the futon, couldn't see me. I thought Erebos might bark at the window and blow my cover, but Wendi had given him a bone she pulled from her purse. She must have had a special night planned for Pan and didn't want any distractions.

I felt bad about spying on Pan. I was mad and disappointed, but my loyalty ran deep. He'd made sure of that when he took me. I thought about my first night in Neverland and how uncertain I'd been of my place with the other lost bois. But I knew, for the first time, when I was under Pan's boot, that I was where I belonged. Watching Mommy and Pan, I realized that I had become one of those bois who'd spied on my most private moments when I first came to Neverland, watching me from their hammocks, sizing me up. Their eyes had glinted in the weak street light that pushed through the very same filthy windows that I now, all these years later, looked through. I saw Wendi tighten her apron strings, reapply her lipstick, and run red nails through her long hair. A Mommy's motions. Pan sat on the futon, Tink perched on his shoulder and picking at his hair. I thought I saw a flash of silver in her beak, but I'm sure it was just the light. Pan's eyes never left Wendi. He was as devoted a boi to her as I was to him.

The night I gave myself to Pan, he left me alone in that hammock. I didn't take my jeans off, and he didn't try to stay. I throbbed against the ropes. I had sworn my allegiance to

Pan in blood. It would not be the last time, but that's the
night I will always remember, because he took me with him.
My two stars, birthed in a burst of blood at the tip of his
knife on my right shoulder, shot pain through my body like
I'd never felt before. I was home. I was Pan's lost boi.

From my spot on the dumpster now, I spied as Wendi
gave herself another once-over in the cracked mirror. She
crossed the room and perched next to Pan, stockinged leg
draped over the futon edge, torn from snagging fingernails
and fence tops. Wendi's scuffed heel dangled, clinging to her
toe. I ground myself against the ridges on the dumpster's lid;
I couldn't help myself, even if it makes me sound like a peep-
ing Tom. I promise it didn't feel that creepy. It was hot and
forbidden, watching Mommy and Pan. His hands rounded
her hips, fist clenching the knot of her apron strings, pulling
up the gingham fabric of her dress to get to her. I should have
looked away.

Pan took Wendi there on the futon, his filthy hands disappearing into her. She was beautiful as she surrendered to him,
but it was Pan I couldn't look away from. He was fucking her
hard, the muscles in his right arm flexing under tattoos and
track-mark scars. I loved his arms with their ropes of muscles
that held me down, choked me out, or helped me up. My eyes
had been locked on the place where wrist met grrrl, and then
I saw his face, sweat dripping from his temples, contorted into
a pained look I didn't recognize. Rivers of tears mixed with
the sweat. Pan doesn't cry; he tells us so. Wendi's eyes were

closed, her head thrown back, sweat pooling in the hollow of her throat, her hands clenched into fists. I've fucked her enough to know that she was close. Out of respect, I didn't want to look at Pan's face, but there was a burning I couldn't avoid. And then his green eyes, glassy with tears, met mine. I moaned. Wendi came with an earthquake-tremor and a cry so loud it drowned mine. I didn't understand what was happening to me or Pan or Wendi or the bois—any of us.

I flattened myself lower on the dumpster, but I didn't have to peek through the window to know that Wendi was nestled into him, her hands playing with the short hairs at the base of his neck. She wanted to seduce him. I'd heard her talking about us, about their bois. She didn't include him as a boi. Wendi discussed our training. I knew I should probably not be listening to this part especially, but I didn't want to leave. Wendi spoke about our future. Her language was careful but firm, and she wanted Pan to take a firmer hand with us. She wanted less unplanned battles, more structure. She said, "Structure is what little bois need."

Pan had been silent as Mommy spoke of the leather bois she would polish us into, the fine representatives of leather community we would be, how it was their responsibility to raise the family right so that we could go out into the world, so that we could make them proud.

"But being Daddy to these bois...it's just a game, just pretend. Right, Wendi?" Pan asked.

I pulled my hands under my chest to keep my heart from

banging against the dumpster lid, and I peered up through the window. Mommy wiped tears from her face with the corner of her apron, then began to pick at the fraying edge, scraping off clumps of mascara. At first I thought the conversation was over, but then, so quiet I could hardly make out her words, she pleaded, "But these bois, they belong to us, to you and me?" Her voice trailed off into an accidental question mark.

I saw Pan shake his head but couldn't make out his words. Wendi wanted us to be a family, not a feral pack. Like any good Mommy, she wanted to tame and housebreak all of us, even Pan. But we were wild and vicious, and that's what always made us real.

"What do you really want me for?" Wendi finally whispered, crumpling into the corner of the futon, as far away as she could get from Pan. This was not what she had run away for. There was a coldness in her voice that was new.

Pan pulled himself to his fullest height, straightened his binder and T-shirt, and looked directly into her eyes. "I want to be the most devoted boi, Mommy!"

Tootles' Story

I rejoined the bois but didn't breathe a word of anything that I had seen or heard. That would have been even more dishonourable. Besides, I didn't want to know any of it.

Pan had brought a Mommy to take care of us, but mostly to tell us stories. It was her stories that Pan had first fallen for, and every night, after we climbed into our hammocks, she told us stories that were dark and yet beautiful. Wendi could string words together into feelings in our fucked, damaged boi bodies and make them into bodies we wanted to think about, be in. Instead of being embarrassed, us bois began to hope her next story would be about us, and not a poem about femme solidarity among the Mermaids, or worse, about one of the other bois. Never before had there been such competition or jealousy between us. Before Wendi, we'd been a unit of Pan's sworn bois. Mommy was slowly pulling us apart, calling us out in turn, and writing about each of her bois as though we were individuals. She articulated John Michael's wit, Curly's humour, or the way she felt when I wrapped my hands around her waist. Wendi had stopped going to the open mic since she came to Neverland, but she performed for us in the kitchen. Pan, of course, still liked to listen to her stories—though like the rest of us bois, he liked them best when they were about him. He tolerated stories about his bois, laughed as she read tales about the Mermaids, and punched walls when, on rare occasions, she shared anecdotes about parents and grownups, about life before Pan. She hadn't forgotten where she came from, and Pan couldn't seem to make her.

I don't know what got into Wendi. Perhaps she was punishing Pan for not being the kind of boi she wanted, but one evening, she announced that she would be telling us a story. All us bois kneeled around her, rowdy and boasting to each other that surely the story would be about us. But Mommy's story was about Mr and Mrs Darling and their house. It was about her school, the GSA, and the college she was to have attended. She talked of a world so foreign it might as well have been outer space to us bois, except to John Michael. Once, I punched the pretentious little snot when she said she knew the Darlings. I don't know why I hit her, but I just didn't like her knowing more about Wendi than I did. And I didn't want her to have had another life before Neverland. I was no one before Pan.

Wendi loves a happy ending, and she'll do anything to get

one. All her stories, no matter how gritty, must end happily. On this night, Wendi was telling us about her life before she ran way with Pan, before I shot her, before Pan tied the apron around her waist, before she was my Mommy. I understood why Pan locked himself in the bathroom and punched the walls. He hated stories like this—stories without us, stories about the kind of grrrl Wendi had been and the kind of woman that she was supposed to grow into.

Mommy was breaking the rules. Had she been anyone else, I would have punished her myself for such an infraction. She wanted us to feel sorry for the Darlings, for these grownups. She was asking us to think of how they must have felt the night that she and John Michael went out the window with Pan, the night that she came to us. I crossed my arms across my chest. Washington had flown down and was perched on my hand, but I refused to laugh at his antics and scowled as Mommy continued her story.

"Think of how afraid they must have been when in the morning they found our beds empty. They tried so hard to be parents to us, and look at how we repaid them." If Pan hadn't been punching holes in the bathroom wall, he would have interrupted Wendi by reminding her that the Darlings couldn't have been devoted parents, as she and John Michael had never shown up on the missing persons/runaway flyers that the police hand out on the stroll.

All the bois looked at each other, exchanging worried glances. We had all run away, all fallen out of our prams, and chosen to live without parents. Some of us had been forced to run from social services, dodging case managers and parole officers. Others were never followed. We survived however we needed to. We'd been everywhere and nowhere, and loved, fucked, and fought with equal ferocity. How dare anyone, even our Mommy, dredge all this up? There are things best left underneath the sediment in which we anchor ourselves. I saw tears in the eyes of Curly and the Twins, and that made me want to take Wendi over my knee, no matter how disrespectful that would have been. I hated her for starting this story, for suggesting an alternative, something that could possibly be different. I hated Pan most for not being here to stop her.

"Don't stories have to have happy endings? The story of the Darlings seems so sad!" one of the Twins finally said. I almost punched him to keep myself from crying, but then I saw the warmest smile cross Wendi's face. This was not a game to her, but as real as Neverland all around us.

"Stories are more complicated than that. Some pieces are happy, and sometimes, in order for a happy ending to come, someone else's life gets destroyed or changed. Sometimes it's too early to tell. Mrs Darling told me once that she would keep a window open for me, always ..." Wendi trailed off and seemed momentarily lost in her own thoughts.

Lost bois didn't have mothers with open windows. We'd fallen from our prams because anything was better than where we were. Even Pan never really knew where I'd come

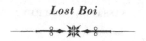
from before he found me in that diner. I'd never spoken to Pan or anyone about what happened to me before I fell from my pram.

I left when I was young—too young. We all do. I left when it was bad, but it could have gotten worse, and it would have. I left before anyone remembered that I would someday grow up. I went looking for my people. I knew what I was back then, or at least some of it. I used every dime I'd saved from babysitting and bought a bus ticket to NYC. You don't need ID to get on those buses; you can just step on and disappear down a highway. There's no way to track you. I'd heard there were gay people in New York. I figured someone would take me in, help me out.

When I got to the city, I saw swarms of people in the Port Authority, an angry hornet's nest of grownups too busy with jobs and money, staring at newspapers and buzzing pagers. I felt dizzy, knowing this was not the life for me. I'd heard there were gays in the Village, so I spanged a little in the station until I had enough coins to buy a subway token downtown. Back then, I looked clean enough that gullible grownups believed my story about being on a school trip and having lost my wallet and trying to get back home.

The train was like a monster filled with grownups. I tried to blend in, but didn't need to worry because no one paid attention to anyone but themselves. People in the Village were worse. They were gay but still grownups. They didn't want me. I tried to ask a guy at a pizza shop if I could wash dishes in exchange for a slice. It seemed like a reasonable offer, and I wasn't entirely expecting him to say yes (after all, I was used to being disappointed by grownups), but I didn't expect him to chase me out of his shop with a broom, yelling that I was a filthy punk dyke and he didn't want me around.

I didn't know what to do. This wasn't at all how I had pictured New York on that long bus ride or in the years I'd spent planning my escape. I wanted to give up, to go "home," but there was nowhere go back to. I sat across from the bar where the gay riots happened, thinking maybe it would give me luck, but I dozed off. When I jerked awake, the couple of bills that had been at the top of my cup were missing. There were more coins and a business card. I almost threw it out, but the rainbow on the back caught my eye. The card was for a gay community centre. For the first time since I stepped off that bus, I was filled with hope.

I slipped in the front door of the community centre and washed myself up in the bathroom, hoping to look better before talking to anyone. The volunteer receptionists were perky queens. I smiled big; I wanted them to like me. They directed me to the back, where they said I could fill out a membership form for the youth program.

I was so green then, it didn't even occur to me to lie. I wrote my real age, answered all the bullshit questions about where I had come from. Had I ever been in a hospital? Did I want to kill myself? Did I use drugs? They asked useful stuff too, like my PGP and how I identified. I handed the clipboard of completed forms back to the lady behind the youth program desk and sat flipping through gay magazines, grinning and thinking to myself how lucky I was to finally be with my people. I started getting nervous when the receptionist looked through my intake and scowled. She picked up the phone and spoke in a whisper, occasionally looking over at me.

Another lady came and took me into a room. No one listened to me—they didn't want to hear how much safer I was now that I was on my own. They just wanted to cover their own asses. They said it was their responsibility as the grownups. I hated them. They left me in a little office with some pity food, a peanut butter and jelly sandwich that tasted as bad as the food I'd gotten in the hospital when, last time, I'd tried a different way to run.

No one stopped me when I opened the door and walked out. The social worker who was trying to turn me in must have been in some back office. No one else noticed or cared as I walked down the stone steps of the gay centre, past the billowing rainbow flag. These were not my people after all. This was not my home.

That night, I met a grrrl. She was working on a street I wandered down. I couldn't believe that such a beautiful grrrl would talk to a boi like me. *Maybe New York isn't so bad after all*, I remember thinking to myself. She told me how to get to The Pier. Told me to wait for her. I don't know why I listened; back then I wasn't much for taking orders from anyone. I guess I was lonely and hadn't really talked to anyone in a long time, and she was beautiful. I waited on a bench until she came. She told me her name was Paris. Paris and I talked on the bench until morning, while all around us kids vogued, dipping and spinning, with only the stars watching on. When the sun started to shine over the Hudson River, I brushed a braid out of her face and leaned in for a kiss. She stopped me.

"Be careful, boi. Don't you remember what I just told you? I'm as toxic as that water." Her eyes lifted off me and onto the churning brown water in which soda cans, dirty diapers, and candy wrappers floated. I gently turned Paris's chin back to me and looked long and hard into her brown eyes. I wanted to tell her everything—about the hospitals and their cold-handed doctors, about the drugs that weren't working any-more to help me forget everything that came before. I wanted to say, "I know what I'm doing; we'll be careful. I'll take care of you always." But instead I kissed her more softly than I'd ever kissed a grrrl. I was so young.

We kissed for a long time, moving from bench to bushes. I laid my coat out to give her somewhere soft, and she pulled some condoms from her purse. We were careful, but I was mostly worried about finding a way to make her feel as beau-tiful as she looked to me. I promised her so much: that we would get an apartment, that I would buy her dresses and dinners out, and that one day I would take her to Paris the city, her namesake. She'd chosen it because it was beautiful and fancy and romantic. I promised that I would kiss her under the Eiffel Tower.

A month later, she was gone. One night, she didn't come back from work. I waited on our bench until morning, then searched everywhere from Christopher to West 4th and all the way to Union Square. The other grrrls said she'd gone with a man in a big sedan. We never found her.

I was lost. I tried more drugs, harder drugs, but nothing helped. I wanted to break the face of every shop owner, every faggot sitting at a café, every dyke barista that wouldn't give me the bathroom key to go piss. I think that's when I decided that I would dedicate everything I had to kids like her, kids like us, because it was clear that all these yuppie gays didn't get it. But in that moment, I couldn't do anything that wasn't destructive. I was too hurt, too broken. I had to get out.

I hopped a freight with some kids I found in Tompkins Square Park. I didn't like them a whole lot, but they'd been on the trains before. You have to be careful with trains, and with het punks. They thought I was a real boy and were always fucked-up enough not to notice anything different. Before we left town, I stole a book about Joan of Arc from a library in the West Village. I thought that was funny, but thankfully none of the kids I was travelling with got the joke.

The trains were scary and dangerous, and if you aren't careful moving around, you can fall and get caught and dragged. The guards are allowed to shoot to kill if they see you "trespassing." The punks I was with kept talking about how it didn't used to be that way, but I thought they were full of shit, because they weren't much older than me but were acting like they had been around forever. I had to always act tough. It was lonely, because the het punks were trashed the whole time, and I was trying to cut back. Somewhere outside of Gainesville, I gave myself a shitty stick-and-poke of the Eiffel Tower. We landed in New Orleans, having rejected Georgia, Florida, and some other states along the way. I fell in love right away with the look of the city and all that wrought iron—hard lace, I called it. The only grrrls I like are hard, so I decided that maybe that city could be my lover for a while. She was real good to me, until, of course, she wasn't, and I left town. I didn't know where I was going, but it didn't take long for Pan to find me in the diner, and, well, you know the rest.

Maybe Pan felt it wouldn't be fair for him to critique Wendi's stories, but it was when she told those stories of life before him that he most regretted having tied her apron strings and wished he'd not just handed his bois to her. It's not that he had lost us, but now we belonged to both of them; a power struggle between them was inevitable. Pan made his displeasure known, but he was a boi of his word; he couldn't stop what was already in motion. I certainly couldn't have pictured what was to come; I don't think even Pan could have imagined it.

Wendi spoke again of how kind the Darlings had been to her, how different they were than those in the other homes where she had been placed. Now John Michael was scarcely paying attention and listened without recognition, as though, like us, she was hearing a bedtime story. Wendi had been a good grrrl, a role model, and she'd led John Michael here ... for what? Love? That wasn't panning out as she'd planned. Wendi sat on the futon in the very same spot where I'd seen Pan break her heart. She used the corner of an apron to wipe her eyes.

"I know she keeps the window open for me, I know she does. I know I wasn't just a cheque to cash; she really loved me," Wendi whispered, more to herself than to any of us. I was confused and angry that she was speaking so much about mothers, but sad to see her eyes fill with tears. Despite the makeup and new clothes, despite knowing her as my Mommy, Wendi was the little grrrl whom Pan had rescued, the little grrrl I'd almost destroyed when, in all her innocence, she crawled through the broken glass into Neverland.

It was almost as though Wendi couldn't handle the sadness of mothers and homes lost in addition to her disappointment about Pan. Her powder was cracking and her lipstick smeared from where she'd wiped snot with her balled fists. Wendi trembled but pulled herself up and straightened her dress, took a lipstick tube from her bra and applied more red to her lips, followed quickly by a flask. There was an edge to Wendi's voice, raw from tears and whiskey.

Pan, who had joined us as Wendi's tears began to fall, started to mock her. "You think mothers are sweet and loving?" Pan jeered. "You think they should be cherished and trusted? Believe me, you're wrong. Just wait—you'll see."

Pan had never spoken about his own past before he'd fallen from his pram. None of us had any idea how old he was or where he had come from. He still kept those secrets guarded, but did let slip that one time, when he returned to the place where he had fallen from his pram, he found that his mother had closed the window on him. The window was not only closed but locked. She had disowned him, forgotten him, and moved on. Thick bars had been installed and, Pan added quickly, there was another child sleeping in the bed that had once been his.

Curly started to cry. I think he still hung onto a dream about the inherent goodness of mothers and having a Mommy was wonderful for him—and triggering. I felt sorry for him, not angry. I remembered the promises I'd made to protect not just us lost bois but all the runaways, the throw-aways. I remembered what it was like to feel completely alone on the streets of New York—and even more alone when I first realized that I had to run, when I first knew that mothers couldn't be trusted. As I saw his eyes get wet, I reached over and grabbed his hand. Pan's eyes met mine as I whispered:

"Curly, we're fine without mothers, we're lost bois. We've built our own family, chosen one another, given oaths in blood to each other. We belong to each other now. Those bad people we were born to can't hurt us now."

That wasn't just a story I told him to stop his tears; I really believed it. I still believe it. Pan smiled at me. It was the first time in a long time I felt really connected to him. It was almost like the old days—he and I against everyone. I remembered how simple it had felt when it was just us, before I became Wendi's boi too and back when Hook didn't take as much of Pan away from us. Lost in my memories, I didn't notice Wendi's crumpled face and the way my words were the final wave to knock her down, swirling in the fast current.

John Michael had watched silently. She was coiling green rope and whispering to one of the Twins about a battle she planned to have with Jukes. She didn't care about Wendi's story. It seemed as though Neverland had become part of her after all, and she, who could best identify with Wendi's story, wasn't interested. Mommy noticed and covered her eyes with the chipped tips of her fingernails. Everything was unravelling for her.

Pan left to see Hook and said he wouldn't be back until late. The other bois started to get up and walk away. I watched Mommy for a while as she stood in the bathroom, door ajar, and fixed her face. Then she sat on her bed. She was the only one of us who didn't sleep in a hammock. I carefully moved toward her, dropped to my knees, and crawled into her lap.

I didn't for a moment regret that I had reminded Curly of our magic, that I had stopped his tears and made him remember the family we had, which was far more important than losing himself in sadness or fear or anger because somewhere, some woman who'd pushed him out of her cunt didn't have a window open waiting for his return. But I hadn't intended to hurt Wendi. She came from a different place with different experiences. She needed to hold onto the belief that she could crawl back through that window, that she could go back and regain her life. I also knew that Wendi didn't disagree with me entirely. For her, it was just more complicated, not as black and white. She valued the world of the grownups, but she also wanted to be our Mommy. The bonds we'd formed and the promises we pledged were as real to her as they were to us. Through Wendi's sweet touch, I had learned the difference between Mommies and mothers. The latter I still knew I could do without, but the former— oh god help me, I had become such a Mommy's boi, and I wanted and needed her more than I ever had before.

We sat quietly on her bed for a while, just Mommy and me. She stroked my hair, which I had, at her request, grown longer. Mommy pulled me tightly to her. "Close your eyes," she purred in my ear. I was a good boi and did what Mommy told me. Please don't misunderstand; I was a willing participant. I wasn't coerced. I took responsibility for the choices I made. Pan taught me that too. It's a good rule.

In her story, Mommy pulled me through the window. We were in her world now, and her voice made it all come alive. She was standing in a kitchen, her kitchen. I was at a table, her table, a pretty vintage one, all shiny aluminum and pink, sparkly Formica. In the story, I was writing an essay, surrounded by textbooks. Mommy walked toward me, holding a clean white plate piled high with chicken, potatoes, corn, salad—all my favourite foods. The plate was for me. "Mommy's smart boi," she said proudly, ruffling my hair as

she placed the plate before me. Her story was so strong that my nose tickled with the scent of fried chicken. It seemed like I could eat those smells. She fed me.

Don't think I've gone soft. Mommy's fantasy wasn't about a full belly or plates without chips. The world Mommy painted was bigger than that, full of questions that I couldn't answer, but was starting to want to.

Pan saved us bois when he could, in the only way he knew how, but I wanted to do more. I'd been thinking a lot about the different ways I'd seen bois pass through here with all their broken dreams. I thought about the evil grownups, the social service workers, the people we all had run from. I started to wonder if there was a way to do that work right. Was there a way to be a responsible grownup, the kind who could actually save kids like us, especially the young ones?

I told Mommy about the promises I'd made to myself so long ago about helping other runaways. I even told her about Paris and pulled up my jeans to show Mommy the faded Eiffel Tower on my ankle. Mommy didn't laugh. I thought she would, but she didn't. She told me that I was a good boi, a strong boi, and that I could do just about anything I wanted. I asked if that meant that I could be an astronaut. I always have been a little bit of a smartass, and when things get intense I make jokes. Mommy laughed and said she wasn't sure about that, but she was certain that if I wanted to care for kids like us, I could find a way to do that—my way, a different way—and that I would be very good at it. Then she told me more about the little house we could have, our magic place right in the middle of the grownup world. She said that no matter how grownup I became, I would always be her boi, and she would always be my Mommy and tuck me in at night.

This was our little secret, this story, this game that Mommy and I played alone, and it seemed more real than any of the fantasies we'd written about where we'd come from. This was really about me and the kind of life that I could have with Mommy. I never told Pan about this special Mommy/boi time. He didn't want to know the details of other bois' dynamics with his Mommy. It was a mistake, but none of us could see that far ahead.

Since her arrival, Wendi convincingly fought against how black and white Pan made the world seem. Pan always told me that if we left, the magic of leather would be broken, and it didn't live in conferences or play parties. I knew what I was—a boi—and not just in gender. I needed to surrender; I needed the containment and purpose that I found in giving myself over to someone else. I always thought I needed Pan, but maybe it was something else, something bigger than all of us. It makes me sound so broken when I put it this way, but I needed to belong to someone I could depend on.

Wendi told me that I could be Mommy's boi anywhere, even if I was sitting at a boardroom conference table wearing a suit. I made a face with mock retching sounds when she said that, which earned me a slap across the cheek.

"Don't interrupt Mommy—it's rude," she continued. Even if I wore a suit, she started again, I would still be her little boi. The magic that lived in our home would be strong enough to follow me out into the world if I wished to do grownup work, because I could come home to her. I didn't have to stay here and compromise my dreams just to keep the magic alive.

When Wendi told us stories, she liked to keep her hands busy. Sometimes it was with mending or knitting and sometimes it was with me. When we played this game, Mommy's hands wandered through the fly of my worn jeans. She spoke about the life we would have and the places we could visit while she was inside me. Mommy told me that I would be strong enough to survive in that world. "A Mommy's love is always and unconditional," Wendi promised.

I came so hard, shaking and crying. I tried to wipe away my tears on the tattered cuff of my hoodie, but Mommy pulled out of me and grabbed my hand, pulling me to her.

"Let me watch you cry," Mommy whispered, looking me right in the eyes. It was not a request; it was an order. Mommy wanted me to give her everything, wanted to fix it, to make it all better. I began to nuzzle at her breasts. The buttons on her housedress fell open, and my mouth found her nipples. I sucked hard, letting my teeth drag against her. Mommy moaned and laid back against the fine lace pillows we'd gathered from the thrift shop to make her a proper Mommy bed. She grabbed my ass as I filled her. She was so wet, so hungry. She came hard around three of my fingers. I didn't cum. I felt sick when Mommy pulled my face up for a kiss and began to whisper.

"You'll come with me, right, sweet boi? You won't leave me, will you?"

I almost pretended not to know what she meant, but her eyes were filling with tears. The silence closed in. Wendi knew now that Pan would never see the world the way that she did. Her fantasy was over; all she could see now was college, houses, full refrigerators, and clean clothes, all disappearing behind a slowly closing window.

My voice cracked. "Yes, Mommy, if you wish it."

That was it, my fate decided and sealed, but it's not that simple. I was a willing accomplice. I'd be lying if I said I hadn't thought of it before she asked. I was willing to leave it all for the promise of a future I'd never seen. "Give me your knife," Mommy demanded. I handed it over, confused and worried because I felt too exhausted for a blood play scene. But Mommy didn't use the knife on me; she held it firmly in her right hand and aimed the tip at the edge of the green stone, Pan's stone, on her birthstone ring. It took all her strength to pry it out, but when the stone fell out, she looked sadly at the hole, second on the right, next to the empty socket where Pan had pried out Nibs' stone. Wendi sighed, took her black handkerchief from her apron pocket, and wrapped up the little green stone for safekeeping. "It's time to tell the bois," Wendi whispered, squeezing my hand and handing back my knife. There hadn't been time for me to think about anything, and no way to take back what I had already agreed to. I didn't think of Pan. I couldn't let myself think of him, though I knew that soon I would have to.

When the bois came in for dinner, Mommy Wendi's dress was re-buttoned and her lipstick fresh. We sat at the table. Wendi had cooked us spaghetti with a sauce as deep red as clotted blood. That morning, Pan had gone to the Jolly Roger, and he wasn't home yet. Pan and Hook had patched things up after the fight at the Lagoon. Pan didn't even remember the conflict, and Hook grew tired of analyzing Pan's form. They never could stay apart for very long. Pan left Erebos to take care of us. Hook was a cat man, and as good a dog as she was, Erebos tended to chase cats, and that wasn't the kind of battle Pan was in the mood for. Pan sent Tink to Neverland with a message in the late afternoon, telling us to have dinner without him. Wendi read the note and then crumpled it up in her apron pocket. She did not send Tink back to Pan with a reply.

When Mommy had given each boi their dinner, she said, "My sweet bois, I wanted to talk with you alone. I've decided it's time for me to go home." She used that word so casually, I almost changed my mind. Wasn't home here with us? I watched as anger flashed across each boi's face.

Curly was the first to speak. He looked undone by her words, his fists bunched and ready to fight, though Pan's training was too strong, and he couldn't bring himself to swing at Mommy. John Michael looked more lost than ever, uncertain of what was happening. She, more than us, knew what it meant to go back, and when Wendi said that she was going home, that she must go back through the window, John Michael assumed there was no choice but to follow Wendi. The Twins were fiercely angry, however; they grabbed Wendi by her wrists.

"You're not going anywhere," one whispered. The spell looked as though it might be broken. He continued, louder now, to try to rile the rest of the bois.

"We will keep her here. She is our Mommy. Pan promised it."

Wendi was looking at me with those big eyes, and I was lost in the memory of her first night in Neverland, the night that she flew, and of her blood dripping down her leg and onto those pretty white sneakers.

"Tootles, please," she cried quietly.

The memory blinked from my eyes. Wendi looked small—smaller than she'd looked since the night she climbed out her window. She shook the way that she had when she was overdosing on our floor. Above her stood Curly, arms laden with ropes, prepared to do what it took to keep her, his eyes filled with angry tears. He kept repeating, "Everyone always leaves," and, "Mommy can't leave." The Twins now looked scared. John Michael was drunk or high, unwilling or unable to help Wendi. I would have saved her from Curly's ropes myself, but Pan beat me to it. Curly grabbed Wendi's hands and she began to sob. Pan must have come back moments

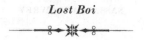
before and overheard what Curly said about forcing Mommy to stay. Maybe he'd heard everything. It would be like him to have listened in. His face was a twisted mess of sadness—knowing that he had lost his Mommy—and anger at seeing his bois behave so badly in his name. One of the most basic rules is that everything is done by free will; no one is ever to be held among us by force.

"Let her go," was all Pan had to say. It was barely more than a whisper, and yet it echoed through all of Neverland, a command that could not be ignored. Curly released Wendi, whose eyes were desperately trying to catch Pan's, but he refused to look at her. Instead, he glanced at me and a sad question and answer travelled unspoken between us.

Wendi hung her head then turned her attention to the bois. I watched as she straightened her dress and sat back down in her chair. Her voice was soft now, like a teddy bear nestled onto a freshly made bed. This was our Mommy speaking, not the Wendi who moments before had told us she was leaving us.

"Sweet bois, my bois, I know you are upset, but that's because you didn't let me finish. I'm not leaving you. Mommy would never leave her little bois." She looked directly at Curly as she said that part. "Shhh, dry those tears," Wendi cooed, looking at the Twins who were huddled together, shaking, eyes wet.

"You could come away with me and crawl through my window into the Darlings' home. I'm sure that they won't mind. You can go to school and get jobs. You'd have a house—and as much ice cream as you could want. I'll never leave you. We can have beautiful lives, help other bois, and do more than hide away in a warehouse..." Although I'd decided to go already, I bristled when Wendi talked so easily about leaving Neverland. How could she do away with who we were, with everything that Pan had built?

Pan. I was suddenly very aware of his presence and of the unfinished business that remained. He stood behind us, straddling a splintered wooden chair and slowly cracking each of his tattooed knuckles, eyes tracing the "LOST BOIS" letters. I regretted my decision then, in part because I feared the unknown that awaited me, but mostly out of honour and duty to Pan, who'd taken me in when no one else wanted me.

It wasn't just Wendi's story or the dreams we'd hatched together that led to my decision to leave. I wasn't alone in wanting to give up, in knowing that what we had wasn't working. Pan had grown more and more distant as his world with Hook intensified, and as he pulled away from us bois, Mommy had become all the more important. We needed Mommy. Us six bois sank to our knees before Pan, eyes pleading.

You can be lonely even when surrounded by those who know you best, those who love you most. My wrist burned, and I looked down at Pan's cuff, where it always was, at the scuffed green leather, padlock, and the metal plaque engraved with the words "Lost Boi." Who was I if not Pan's? How long would it be before he forgot me?

The room was silent. Wendi and us bois looked at Pan, but I couldn't meet his gaze, knowing that if he looked at me, I would come undone. All the bois seemed enchanted with the growing-up world that Wendi promised, the world we had all left and despised. I stared at our boots, at the way Curly's had separated from their soles, Slightly's had duct-tape-wrapped toes, and the Twins, who didn't have boots, wore black skater shoes. It was only John Michael who had nice boots, smartly blacked. They were castoffs from Pirate Jukes, which she'd made some kind of trade for. My eyes travelled over each pair of feet until I reached the ones I knew best, better than my own, the gouged and worn leather that adorned Pan's. While his voice was measured as he spoke, I could see the leather of his boots ripple as he clenched his toes again and again. His boots were tight; I knew it must hurt to strain his feet against the leather and laces. It was the pain that must have kept his voice so calm. The pain must have given him the resolve to say quietly, "You are free to go, if you wish. I won't force a boi to stay."

There was a collective sigh of relief from all the bois, who began whispering quickly about what they must pack, what they would need to begin their new lives. I was ashamed of the bois and of myself. How quickly our whims and allegiances could change! How quickly we could forget that it was Pan who had saved us, Pan we had sworn ourselves to in blood. "Take care of yourselves, and your Mommy," he added without a trace of the anger I expected.

I felt my neck redden, and I knew Pan had finally turned toward me, his best and most loyal boi. "I thought you were different. I thought you were like me and understood exactly what we had built here." Then he turned away.

Wendi grabbed his arm, her red nails wrapping around his wrist. "You can come with us. That's the way I wanted it, the way I imagined it would be. I'll read you stories. We'll have a house together, a life."

Of course, just a few hours earlier Pan had finally broken her heart with his inability to grow up and be the boifriend, Daddy, and egalitarian partner whom Wendi wanted, to fulfill the fantasy she had fallen deeply in love with.

Pan laughed, a scary and hollow laugh. "No, Wendi," he finally said. "Neverland is my home. It always has been and always will be."

Outsiders saw Neverland as a broken-down warehouse filled with furniture that was not worth being pulled from a dumpster, spray-painted walls, and a floor caked with pigeon shit, but Pan saw magic and possibility. This was his world, and there would be no domesticating him. Wendi turned and dried her eyes with the hem of her dress. She loved Pan, that much I knew for certain. We all loved him. I loved Pan deeper than I'd ever loved anyone.

Pan stood next to me, but he had never felt farther away. He hated goodbyes, felt they were undesirable and unnecessary. If you were going away, there was nothing to say. That kind of abandonment was unforgivable, and soon you would

be forgotten. Pan looked at each of us bois in turn and calmly said: "I hope you like growing up."

"Why Are You Really Here without Pan?"

There was a party that night at the Jolly Roger. Despite the hurried plans and packing and arrangements that Mommy was making to take us bois away, it was decided that we should go. Normally, everyone was excited to go to the Jolly Roger parties, especially Pan, but he was still sleeping as we all went out into the night. I didn't want to go without Pan; in fact, I didn't really want to go at all, but there was no disobeying Mommy. It felt strange to walk up to the heavy, red wooden door and pick up the massive, skull-shaped brass knocker, cold and weighty in my hand. The Captain's first mate Smee met us at the door. If he was surprised to see us arrive without Pan, he was well-trained enough to keep it off his face.

Smee led us through the formal entryway with its dark mahogany panelling. We could see into the lush living room filled with red velvet couches and expensive art from the downtown galleries that Hook was connected to. I'd never spent much time in the living areas of the Jolly Roger and wasn't surprised when Smee led us away from that part of the home, down the stairs, and to the dungeon. I could hear a deep thumping beat from surround-sound speakers mixed with the laughter of partygoers and punctuated by the occasional scream. My stomach lurched. I knew I wasn't in the mood for any of this tonight. My thoughts were with Pan, who was probably still sleeping in Neverland instead of here with us. I don't think that the bois really believed that we were leaving. Maybe they thought this was just another one of Mommy's stories. We would battle the Pirates tonight, and tomorrow would be a normal day at Neverland, but I knew it was over between Pan and Wendi, and we were going. I knew too that I should make the most of this night—not that I thought we would be vanilla and simple when we left; I knew we could still have play and live lives of Leather, but we would never again battle Pirates at the Jolly Roger. I hadn't thought it through very well. Leaving Pan still felt unknown, unreal, and yet it was happening.

The Mermaids arrived not long after us, dressed in their finest. I hid in the bathroom, shit-sick with nerves. It's not that I couldn't stay; I knew I could choose to never leave and be like Pan. Perhaps that was the hardest part, knowing that I was choosing to grow up. This was something I wanted, and yet I was fiercely disappointed in myself that my decision hadn't been a more difficult one, that it was so easy to leave my Sir. Of course, it wasn't that I wanted to leave Pan, but I wanted to keep my earlier promise to myself, and saving bois based on Pan's whims and attractions wasn't feeling big enough for me anymore.

I avoided Siren as she entered the party. I wasn't ready to tell her, to say goodbye. It's not like I was physically going far away—just down the tracks, across the Interstate, and up from the river—and it's not that we couldn't still see each other, but even then I knew that we wouldn't. I knew the choice to leave Pan was a choice to leave everything about the life I knew. Siren eventually found me, though; I couldn't hide from her forever. She looked beautiful, her blue hair knotted into a bun with a plastic shark tangled into the centre. I stared at its cheap plastic jaws instead of meeting her eyes. I think Siren knew what was going to happen even before I told her. My voice cracked as I whispered that, if she had time, I needed to talk. She left Kelpie and followed me to a quiet corner where I lost my nerve and leaned in to kiss her. Siren made a move that looked like she was about to step away from me when suddenly I found myself pinned against the wall, her hand wrapped around my jaw, forcing me to meet her eyes.

"What was it you needed to tell me, boi?" she hissed mockingly. I was red and near tears.

I hesitated a moment too long, and then said, "Mommy and I and all the bois are leaving. We're going home with her. I might go to college and get a job and figure out how to save all the lost kids everywhere."

Siren slapped me. She wasn't playing, she was angry. The worst part was that, after the slap, she walked away. I knew better than to follow her, but my eyes couldn't pull away from the seam of her tattered stockings. Leaving hurts. I had never before been the one to abandon someone. It's not as easy as you think.

There was nothing to say to anyone. I felt high—everything was far away and blurry, as though my body was separate from me. I remember walking away, my face stinging. I think I was having a panic attack, so not my style, especially in the middle of a goddamn play party. Hook found me clinging to a banister, sweating and shivering. At first he thought I was being chased by the Crocodile, and I think he was preparing to throw me out of the Jolly Roger. Hook had no patience for the Crocodile. He was terrified of it, knowing all too well how strong it bites, the way it can rip everything from you.

Somewhere between pulling me off the mahogany banister and nearly throwing me out the front door, Hook realized I wasn't swimming with the Crocodile. He steered me into his formal living room and slid the wooden pocket door closed. The red curtains were pulled tightly over the windows, and the room was lit with softly glowing lamps. If I hadn't been panicked, if I hadn't been running away, I would have thought it romantic. Hook laid me down on the plush red velvet couch, propping my boots onto a black pillow before sitting down in a wingback chair. He studied me as I lay in the throes of a huge panic attack. It was embarrassing. Only Pan had seen me in this state before. When I get this far, when the panic winds through me, there's nothing I can do but tremble and cry and let it run its course. I used to think I was going to die when my breathing quickened and my eyes rolled back. It feels like all the lost bois have piled onto my chest and are sitting there, beating on my ribcage.

I'd never been alone with Hook, and I shivered harder. It was obvious what Pan saw in him. I wondered how many evenings they had spent together in this very room, or perhaps they went somewhere more private? How rude and insubordinate I had become to flatter myself so, to think that Hook might look at me with the same starving hunger that crossed his face whenever he was close to Pan.

We sat for a long time as my breathing steadied. Hook said nothing, just watched me, and after a while, I wasn't panicked anymore. Well, I was freaking out, but in a totally different way. I thought of everything Pan had ever told me about Hook, who was the closest thing he had to a Sir, but not really, because they were so evenly matched, because Hook could never own Pan, no one could. I didn't know what Hook had planned for me tonight. I was so tired. I closed my eyes, and when I opened them again, Hook was coiling a beautiful purple rope. He looped it around his hands. My mind was still foggy, and I struggled to piece together his words as he uttered a barrage of questions.

"I think you should fly with me tonight, don't you?

Where's Pan? Little boi, what's this crying about? Where's that Mommy of yours?"

These questions weren't really meant to be answered. It was a cruel, seductive interrogation, where we both knew that I would lose and that I didn't want it to go any other way.

Hook stood and walked a couple of steps across the plush carpeting. He took me into his rope, and I let him. I wanted to lose. I wanted to lose control more than I wanted Hook. It wasn't about hurting Pan. I know how stupid that sounds, given the circumstances. I trusted Hook because he was Pan's best fight, because Pan had lost to him, because Pan wasn't here to take me down, because I knew then that I'd never again find myself under Pan's boots. Hook, true to his reputation for good form, was fast and skilled. I don't entirely remember how it happened, but soon the purple rope was around my chest and hips, and he had me suspended from a point in the ceiling. I laughed at the thought of myself flying over this formal living room. Hook didn't like laughter and punched me hard in the chest. No words, just a look that meant I needed to behave, that I shouldn't anger him. Pan was all about fun; Hook took it all seriously. I was caught in his riptide, and I wasn't fighting against the pull.

I flew that night under the hands of Hook. I knew he was an expert rigger; it's why all the conferences wanted him, why Pan flew under him too. I thought we were going to fuck. Hook had me suspended wearing nothing but my boots and briefs—so different from Pan, who prefers bois to be clothed.

I wasn't sure how I felt about being fucked by Hook and what it would be like for him to slip into one of my holes. I'd never thought about it before, and in that moment, I realized that I wasn't even sure of Hook's preferences, though I was certain I would soon find out.

I felt his palm run the length of my back but stop before he reached the curve of my ass. He left his hand on the small of my back, leaned toward me, and whispered in my ear.

"Why are you really here without Pan?"

I gasped and pulled against Hook's ropes. This wasn't any of Hook's business, and certainly wasn't my place to tell him, but I didn't know how to stop myself.

"I'm leaving Neverland. I'm going home with my Mommy, we all are," I whispered, and then I broke, my tears falling silently to the carpet.

Saved by a Fairy

ook untied me and brought me down to the carpet without speaking a word. What could he have said? I wasn't his boi to praise for answering a hard question or to scold for making the selfish choice to leave. I was a tool, and not a particularly valuable one. I had given Hook what he needed, and he was through with me. He left me on the carpet, crumpled next to my clothes.

I later found out that, after walking away from me, Hook left his own party. It's not far to Neverland. Pan was still there sleeping when Hook pried open one of the big front windows, the one with the broken glass that Wendi had crawled through. Pan slept restlessly in Wendi's big bed, tangled in the sheets, straining against the stained and cigarette-burned cotton. To Hook, he looked like he was fighting sleep, fighting something.

Pan is haunted by his past, by pieces of his life that none of us know and maybe even he doesn't remember anymore, at least when he's awake. In his sleep, Pan fights the memories of everyone who's ever hurt him. Sometimes I would wake up and, from my hammock, see Wendi comfort him. Before Mommy came, none of us knew what to do. My first night with Pan, I'd made the mistake of trying to wake him from a dream and sported a shiner the following week. After that, none of us bois ever tried to wake him. We would roll over in our hammocks, turn on our Discmans, or just plug our ears and dissociate as our Sir whimpered, fought, and lost against something, someone, we couldn't see. We never spoke about it.

Once Mommy came, everything changed. She saw Pan's dark dreams and would take him into her arms, holding and rocking him until he woke. Pan never struck Mommy the way he had me. It was a Mommy's magic. When she chased away his nightmares, Wendi learned that she could be a Mommy not only to Pan but to all us bois. In saving Pan from his nightmares, Wendi realized that she could find a piece of a boi, a shiny, glittery part that no one had touched or ruined, and tuck it into her apron pocket. She learned that she could keep us safe and polish us until we shone. But now, the apron had been untied and left upon the bed. In his sleep, Pan clenched it in his little fist. He was alone.

Hook stood in the doorway, watching as Pan slept. His jeans tightened uncomfortably and he rolled his eyes at himself. This wasn't about sex, and he knew it. Hook wasn't interested in fucking Pan. He watched as the little boi fought sleep.

It wasn't the tangle of sheets that kept Pan's body prisoner, it was the tears that carved rivers on his cheeks. Hook watched Pan, thinking of all the battles they'd had, of all the times he'd been so close to slipping, to letting himself go somewhere he wasn't allowed, where his honour code wouldn't let him go. Hook's eyes travelled down Pan's body to the scuffed and scarred boots of his biggest rival, his deepest love. This was deeper than he'd realized. Hook steadied his breath and focused on the smallness of the boi, the scars on his shoulders visible as the A-shirt he wore was pushed to the side. Pan's back was a starry sky of scars, both those that were cut by bois' knives and the scarred dotting of Hook's own hooks, the ones he'd pierced Pan with and flown him from in the rigging of the Jolly Roger.

Hook walked across the floor, picking his way across the pigeon shit so as not to tarnish his boots. Pan heard the click of those boots on the concrete and sat up in the bed, blinking hard, trying to make sense of what was happening, of who he was, and where he was, and why Hook was in Neverland.

"She's left you, hasn't she? What good is a boi without his Mommy? You finally figured out that you wanted one, brought her here to be with you, and then couldn't keep her," Hook taunted. He reached into the pocket of his leather jacket and pulled out a silver chain and padlock with a skull and crossbones, surrounded by the words "Property of Hook," etched into the metal.

Pan's eyes travelled from the chain to Hook's face, but

stopped before meeting his eyes. Pan was exhausted and confused; everything was falling apart. Neverland couldn't exist without him, and who was he without bois? He looked away from Hook and down to his knuckles at the faded ink. The word "LOST" on his right hand seemed darker and less aged than the ink on his left hand.

He looked around the empty warehouse. Neverland looked dull and tired, as tired as he felt—old, even, though he hated that word. What would it mean to be Hook's boi? They had always been rivals, evenly matched in battle. Could he surrender to such a pretentious prick? Could he submit himself to Hook's old-fashioned protocols? What was left for him if he didn't?

Pan seldom thinks about anything for too long. His world is impulse, passion, and chance. We were gone, and even I had left him. We'd gone away with his Mommy. Pan extended his hand for the collar, not meeting Hook's eyes. Hook pulled the chain away with a laugh and a slap that left Pan's cheek stinging. Of course, protocol. He would not be permitted to touch that which was not his. Instead, Pan lowered his head. He felt the cold metal land on his chest and watched as Hook's boots moved behind him, sensed his hands hovering above his neck, heard the padlock unbolt. At that moment, Tink soared through the window and landed at the nape of Pan's neck where Hook was preparing to lock the collar. Hook tried to shoo her away, but Tink pecked at his hands, and he backed away.

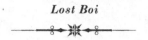

Tink hopped to the floor and caught Pan's gaze before flying up and landing on his head, pecking again and again to wake him up in the only way that she knew how. Hook reached in again with the collar, but Pan shook himself away from Hook's hands.

Hook crossed Neverland without a word. The short-lived fantasy was over. Pan would never surrender to him—Hook didn't need to process the failed collaring to know that. Pan was incorrigible, filthy, and he let a fucking bird call the shots in his life. Despite this, there was still a small part of Hook that wanted Pan, wanted him badly. Wanted those filthy little hands and leather cuff.

Satisfied that Pan was not going to chase after Hook, Tink stopped pecking at her master. His neck was bloody in the spot where the collar would have come together. She'd saved him, and he knew it.

But Pan hadn't forgotten the way the Pirate captain looked longingly at him when one of the lost bois was under his boot, when he had someone quivering and sobbing at the end of a long scene. Pan knew that there was something the Pirate wanted, something he could give, if only Hook could let himself have it. Perhaps all was not lost. Perhaps, Pan realized, he was not entirely alone.

14

The Jolly Roger

don't know how long I stayed in Hook's living room. Probably longer than I should have, but I felt so alone and didn't know where I was supposed to go. Part of me wanted to run back to Neverland, to break my commitment to Wendi, to take back my word and my plans, but I knew that it was too late.

If I walked back into Neverland, Pan would want to take me in. I was his good boi, his best boi. He would remind me of who I was, of everything that we were to each other and all that we'd been through and then he would tell me that it was over. Pan forgives no one. Leaving is the worst offense.

I'd watched it happen before with bois who left, who decided to grow up. They would come crawling back. Sometimes he wouldn't see them, wouldn't even let them in. Other times, he'd grant them permission to spend the night, maybe even give them a hammock. The boi would think that they had won, that they could come back to our world. Then, at breakfast, Pan would break them. Either he would act like they were nothing but an empty chair that he couldn't see, or he'd be confused and vacant when the boi would talk about what his life at Neverland had been like. These bois would walk out the door, dazed and alone, unsure if everything they had experienced here had been real or nothing but a dream. Then there were the bois who fought Pan, who tried to force their way back into his world; they had to be physically thrown out of Neverland. I'll never forget their bewildered faces. I couldn't be one of those bois. I had too much pride. Pride is a weakness. I deserved to have Pan look through me without recognition.

Eventually, I made myself pull on my clothes and rejoin the Pirate party. There was nothing to do but keep my word to Mommy. The party was loud when I hit the play space. I saw bois, Pirates, and Mermaids fucking and battling against the walls and on all the equipment. I didn't see Wendi and figured that she was busy with something—someone, more likely. I didn't go looking. Siren was being fucked by Smee, which pissed me off. What did I care, I told myself; I was the one leaving.

Jealousy aside, I was surprised to see them together, since Smee had always seemed like a gold-star faggot. Shows what I knew. But Smee was a tricky one: he was Hook's right-hand man, his primary partner, and his first mate. They were as inseparable as Pan and I had been. I turned away from their scene. John Michael was kneeling before a raised chair, blacking the boots of Hook's man Jukes. Without really trying, I caught a piece of their conversation, details of an upcoming title-and-sash pageant. John Michael's eyes shone. It was obvious that she was already plotting her next moves, that she would move on just fine without Pan.

I dozed for a while on a leather love seat, then woke with a start and looked around the dungeon. All the bois were tied up with Pirates standing over them. Normally, our battles are more evenly matched, with more switching than one side totally dominating, but the bois knew that this would be their last lost boi/Pirate battle. Smee, who must have finished with Siren, walked toward me. I cocked my head invitingly, not sure what I was up for, but beating on a Pirate seemed like it might feel good, might be an effective way to let myself forget about leaving.

Smee was a good boy—better than me, evidently. Maybe the Pirates had it right all along. They aren't grownups, not really, since they live in a fantasy that adjoins ours, but they aren't as frantic as we are. They have guides, protocols, honour codes, and Hook's lessons about good form, not to mention jobs that mean they can afford new boots and dinner.

Smee was waiting, smiling, watching. I lunged. His reflexes were good and fast and he met me. It felt so good to let our bodies crash into each other, to feel the weight of him smashing into me. We hit hard. This was not for show. The air was knocked out of me when we collided, and we tumbled to the floor on top of one another. The bois and I are all expert wrestlers. Normally it isn't even my kink, but tonight it felt good to struggle with, not against, this Pirate. Smee is a dandy. He works at the vintage hardware shop in the fancy arts district a few streets over. He's a nelly, but tough too. We like each other as much as any lost boi and Hook crewman could. When it's bois versus Pirates, Smee and I usually battle each other. Tonight, he pinned and hogtied me. It had been a fair fight.

All us bois were tied and beaten by the Pirates. I panicked, wanting Pan. It was embarrassing how much I wanted to call out for my Sir, how much I wanted to cry. Thankfully, Smee had stuffed his black handkerchief with the silver skull and crossbones into my mouth. I bit down hard on the cloth, willing the tears not to come and tried to meet the eyes of the other bois. Curly was coming loudly under Cecco; he was not the slightest bit alarmed. Perhaps I was wrong to let panic get the best of me again. Perhaps this was just a friendly ambush.

I saw her first. Mommy Wendi, with her skirt and petticoats around her hips, her arms laced above her head, tangled in a spider web of pink rope. The mascara had run down her round cheeks in dark winding rivers, and I wanted to lick them away, but of course I couldn't move toward her. Hook's left hand was in, to the wrist, and his right one rested almost tenderly on her stomach. I think Smee was trying to get my jeans down, but I wasn't paying attention to him—not resisting but not cooperating either. My attention was on my Mommy, and on Hook. Staring was rude, but I couldn't will

myself to look away, couldn't bring myself to ignore what was happening.

"Looks like you've lost your two stars to the right. How are you going to find your way back to Neverland?" Hook laughed and gestured toward the two stones missing in Wendi's birthstone ring. "You could stay with me and my men," Hook said as he twisted his wrist and pushed deeper into her. Wendi moaned, which wasn't an answer, but Hook was encouraged. "You could be my Pirate Bride. I could be everything to you that Pan can't be. Wendi, I am a man of Leather. Who do you think you are, going out into the world? Do you really think you can keep all your bois clean? You're going to lose them, Wendi. You know what can happen to bois who don't listen to their Mommy, and it's so much harder to make them listen out in the real world. You'll be visiting them in cemeteries and prisons. Stay here, Wendi. I can love you, and you can be our Mommy. Look around, do you see this crew? They have never had a Mommy, no one has ever tucked them in, never told them stories."

Hook's husky voice trailed off. Wendi seemed to be drowning under the weight of his words. Could she stay? Could she build a life here among the pirates? What did Hook know about what Pan had never been able to give her, anyway?

I strained against Smee's grip. I wanted to tell her to say no, but the handkerchief was deep in my mouth. She couldn't belong to Hook, couldn't allow herself to be taken by Pan's greatest battle partner. To do that would be worse than leaving, worse than all of us growing up. Wendi studied Hook's well-built frame, and her eyes came to reset on the intricate tattoo on his left forearm: a skull, a suspension hook, and roses wrapped around the words "Death Before Dishonor."

"Never!" she shouted and strained against her ropes, and then yelled the word "*Red!*" The scene was over. Hook had lost her. His right hand grabbed the ornate handle of a knife from his belt and sliced her ropes, bringing her down to sit on a nearby stool. Wendi rubbed the rope marks on her arms.

Pan had slipped down the stairs without any of the Pirates noticing his arrival. When I saw him, I almost called out, but of course I couldn't, both by training and because of the handkerchief in my mouth. If I had been able to move, I would have to run to him, but his eyes were only on Hook and Wendi. Hook ran his hands through Wendi's hair.

"Are you sure, pretty Mommy?" Hook's voice was flirty and low. Wendi looked so proud and grownup in that moment as she straightened herself to her fullest height and looked up into Hook's dark eyes.

"Sir, I am certain."

I couldn't tell if she was mocking him or employing impeccable manners. Hook cocked his head; he also wasn't certain. "Well, pretty grrrl, you've made your choice, and I wish it were a different one, but I don't force grrrls to do things they don't want."

All the bois and Pirates had stopped mid-fuck or battle

and were paying attention to Wendi and Hook's exchange. When Hook knew he had everyone's attention, his voice changed, growing cold and serious.

"Wendi, have you learned nothing in your time here? Have you learned nothing about the price of the decisions we make? Did Pan teach you nothing of consequences?"

Pan! I had almost forgotten that he was in the dungeon, for I knew he would never have crept away, especially when he heard what Hook was saying.

"These bois are no longer your responsibility," Hook continued. "These lost bois shall become my new crew." At that moment, Hook turned his attention to us. "I know that you have failed your Sir, that you have removed your cuffs and broken your oaths, that you have decided to follow your Mommy to her home. She has tempted you with promises of a home and full bellies. She's sold you cake and clean sheets, but has not spoken much of what will come with those luxuries. You will grow up. You will go to offices and schools. Sure, you can still be perverts, but it will be much harder to stay true to who you are in a world that will want to marry you off and make you nice lesbians." We all winced. "Stay with me. Become part of my crew. Notice how well cared for they are." Hook poked Jukes, who had been flogging John Michael, in his round stomach.

"I'm a good Captain, and you will be well cared for if you join my crew. What do you say, bois?"

It was a tempting offer to spend forever with the good

parts of our world, the safe and good parts, but also be able to ignore the painful bits, the ways in which Pan had let us down, the ways that we had abandoned him. The bois all looked at me. Some things don't change—they looked to me as Pan's best boi. I flushed, thinking of what I had thrown away, what I had become, and most of all, how I had let Pan down in ways I could never take back. Hook nodded in our direction, and Smee pulled the handkerchief from my mouth. I ran my tongue across my chipped teeth's sharp edges and looked Hook in the eye.

"No, I will never be yours. I belong to my Mommy."

I think I surprised Hook there. He seemed confused that we had all turned him down. The lost bois all nodded as I finished speaking. My eyes scanned the room of bound bois and came to rest on John Michael. I was surprised to see her nodding in agreement. I didn't think she would turn down the chance to be a Pirate. I asked her about it later, and she said there was part of her that wanted to join Hook's crew, but she'd been afraid to break rank with the rest of us bois, and most of all, she hadn't wanted to disappoint Wendi.

Hook was used to getting his way, used to unquestioning submission from his crew. To have Wendi and all us bois refuse his offer was unexpected. "If that's what you wish," was all he replied. He walked to the other side of the dungeon through a small, almost invisible door in the dark panelling, that I'd never noticed. The bois and Pirates returned to their good-natured battling, and Wendi joined Kelpie and some of

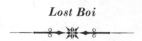
the other Mermaids, who had given space to this scene and set themselves up on plush couches and spanking benches.

I walked toward the dark corner where I had last seen Pan. He was still there, pressed between a wooden chest and the wall. He tensed, then relaxed when I approached. Pan whispered, not so much to me but to himself, or perhaps to something, someone much bigger, "It's always just me and Hook." It was almost an oath, and then a wide smile crossed his face. I had never seen Pan so happy. I didn't know what he had planned, but it seemed he'd already forgotten that I mattered. He had moved on to bigger battles.

15

"It's Always Just Me and Hook"

"Why is everyone breaking all the rules?" Pan later recalled having wondered as he quickly made his way to the Jolly Roger. He couldn't shake the memory of seeing Hook in Neverland, where he'd never been before. There were rules in their—not love, not romance—whatever it was, a connection deeper than there are words for. Hook had stood there with that collar, inside Neverland, interrupting all the rules of good form. Pan decided to go to the Jolly Roger to find Hook, to try to make sense of at least one part of his life.

First it was Wendi with her ideas, her goals of growing up, her plans for worldly success and clean sheets. Maybe bringing her to Neverland had been a bad idea, but no—he had wanted a Mommy, and there was nothing wrong with that. The whole point of Neverland was to exist outside the rules, to make new ones and not be confined, like Hook, so bound to his rules of who you had to be in order to live in Leather.

Pan knew that life could be much more complicated than that; life could look different, feel different. That's why he had built his own world, and one of the first rules he made for himself was never to look back, never regret, and never, ever apologize for finding pleasure. No, Pan thought to himself, Wendi had not been a bad choice. But breaking his own rule, Pan regretted not having paid better attention to his bois, to our care, and the way that he had given us freely to Wendi. Pan later told me that he hadn't ever considered the chance that one day she might order us away and that we would follow the sweet lady, her soft voice, her promises.

The front door of the Jolly Roger was open when Pan arrived. There was no need to knock or announce himself. The plush entrance hallway seemed to swirl around his dusty boots. Pan ducked into Hook's living room, but Hook wasn't sitting in his chair as Pan had imagined he would be. He saw a purple rope near the couch left in a messy heap, not nicely coiled as Hook required.

"The accidental carelessness of a lost boi for certain, but which one?" Pan wondered to himself. I'm so grateful that I wasn't there to see his face as he fingered the soft rope, bringing it to his nose to inhale. It wasn't until much later that I had to endure a confrontation. He knew all his bois better than we knew ourselves. Pan could identify which boi had left behind a filthy sweat sock or used rope. Pan rubbed his eyes. "No tears, not now, not ever," he swore to himself as his nose found me on the rope and he bit his lip and fixed his

gaze on the hooks in the ceiling that had held me not long before.

Pan was about to drop the rope where he'd found it, but instead he coiled it up perfectly. Never let anyone say he was leader of the lost bois for lack of options, skill, or training. This was the right and best choice, he told himself, this life that he had sworn himself to uphold. Pan left the neatly coiled rope on Hook's chair before going in search of the Pirate Captain.

Downstairs, he first saw his bois occupied in deep battle with Pirates, and this made him smile, for the bois all fought well, showing our training to advantage in the way that he taught us to breathe through the pain, to guide another not just through it, but into it. No matter what side of the battle we were on, we were doing him proud. Then Pan remembered that we were not his anymore, and his eyes scanned the room, looking for our Mommy, knowing that she would lead him to Hook. Pan knew Hook might have had a sweet spot for destroying bois, but he lusted for a Mommy.

They had once even talked of it. Hook listened longingly as Pan described the way that Wendi tucked us all in at night and the special attentions she gave him when she reached his hammock. Hook's eyes glistened with desire when Pan said that, afterwards, he had never slept so peacefully. That was the only time they spoke of Wendi, not long after Pan brought her to Neverland.

Pan entered the basement and waited silently until, one by one, we all turned down Hook's offer of a life of Piracy.

Pan was proud of our refusal; if we couldn't be his, if we were going to leave him, then at least we were acting honourably in refusing Hook. Maybe Pan thought we would change our minds, but he knew us better than that, knew that we could not reverse course. But he hadn't come to the Jolly Roger for us; he needed Hook.

When everyone had left or turned their attention back to battle, Pan cracked open the door to Hook's study and slipped inside. The room was dark, beautiful, and filled with antiques. A huge wooden desk carved with ornate depictions of sailors, mermaids, and sea monsters dominated the centre of the room. Hook sat at it, his back to the door, his head resting in his gold-ringed fingers. Pan wasn't certain, but he thought the Captain might be crying.

Pan silently crossed the room on the soft carpet. It was the sound of his gasp that gave him away. Upon Hook's desk lay a used syringe. Pan knew that Hook had long run from the Crocodile, his biggest foe and fear. He'd never forgiven Pan for having fed him to it so long ago—it had changed every-thing—and Pan now regretted that act. He had not foreseen that Hook would forever find himself chased by the Croc. Hook forbade his crew from going near Gator and had even thrown overboard many a crew member who'd tried to sneak a swim with the Crocodile. Hook said that he had time only for pirates who were committed, who could serve him com-pletely, and who were not distracted by lust for something besides their place in his crew.

Pan now stood directly in front of the desk, and Hook looked up at the boi through his wet, laced fingers. Hook's cap lay among the paperclips and condoms on the desk. Hook's leather jacket hung on the back of his chair, and the right arm of his shirt was rolled up. Pan's eyes rested on his forearm and the old-school tattooed lettering, "DEATH BEFORE DISHONOR."

"Have I ever told you about good form?" Hook slurred, eyes fluttering. Pan only nodded.

"Good form is everything. It's all I've ever cared about, all that has ever mattered to me. It's how I was brought out, how I was raised by the great Leathermen who came before. I have tried to guide my crew the best I could, to keep them safe, to give them a home, which they never had before. You've done the same thing for your lost bois." Hook paused. "But you have always done it wrong."

Pan bristled but for once bit his tongue and let Hook continue.

"I always thought you were missing something big, something important. You never understood how serious Leather is. I tried to teach you this, to bring you to my side, but you didn't learn!"

Pan could hold back no longer. "If I'm so bad, if I have such poor form, then why do you want me so much?" he asked. "I don't mean all our battles—I'm talking about today! You came to Neverland. You stood before me, offering me a collar. You wanted to own me. Why? Why would you try to take me and then turn and try to take my bois? I'm the one who should be drowning. My lost bois and my Mommy have all left me today, and now this? What's your game, Hook?"

Hook sat quietly for a long moment, head bobbing. Pan recalled the night many years earlier, when they first battled. He had been so young, so lost, too lost to even take pride in it, too lost to band together with anyone. Pan had gone to the dungeon in search of adventure. He wanted to fly, and the queer at the door pointed him to the man in impeccable leathers with a hook tattooed on his forearm who stood coiling rope beside a package of hooks fresh from the autoclave. Hook put stars of a different kind on Pan's back that night; he took him into the rafters and beyond. Hook hurt Pan, and Pan fell in love, in a way—the closest to love he'd ever gotten. That night, Pan followed Hook to the Jolly Roger and fed him to the Crocodile with no thought of the future, of what might become of this man who had gotten deep into him in a way that no one else could.

Hook looked up at Pan, his pupils tiny pinpricks, and said, "I wanted you because I can't let you have me."

Pan paled and leaned against the back of an upholstered armchair, steadying himself.

"But I'm a failure," Hook said. "I've fought for perfect form, demanded it of my crew, and taught workshops about it, but I've never achieved it, never. I've fought it all along, but I can't shake you when I close my eyes. No matter how loyal my crew, I would trade them all to be yours, to feel your cuff lock around my wrist. To know that you would care for me, could hold and contain all of me. I've tried so hard to hate you, but I couldn't. Even after you fed me to the Crocodile. I tried to collar you because if you were mine, if I controlled you, I could kill the part of me that wanted to be under that filthy boot of yours. I thought, maybe, I could clean you up. I thought I could get rid of the parts of you I want so much."

Pan focused on his breath as he listened to his most trusted opponent admit this weakness. How evenly matched he had always thought they were. Pan thought of the collar he had turned down just hours before, the way it had glistened in the streetlight pushing through Neverland's dirty windows. He thought with grief how close he had been to letting Hook lock it around his neck. Pan straightened himself and took three steps to the desk, holding Hook's eyes the entire time, not allowing him to look away.

Pan grabbed Hook's wrist. "Let me get you to the hospital. This isn't how it is going to end." Pan knew what was happening, and he didn't have any Naloxone. Pan swallowed hard, before continuing, looking Hook right in the eye: "Boy, don't make me force you."

Hook winced, pulled his hand away, and laughed a sad laugh that broke into sobs. "See? You and your impeccable form, even now. You would have me? Disgraced shell of the man I've become? Goddamn it, Pan, does nothing bother you? Do you not ever falter? No, I will drown tonight. I am tired, boi, so tired of running. I'm tired of hiding. I can't do this anymore. The Crocodile will finally take me."

Pan took the Captain's final order and called no one. He stayed with Hook, his oldest friend, until the end. It was the first order he'd ever obeyed.

Afterward, Pan wanted nothing to do with us bois, but he allowed Wendi to hold him tightly as the tears came. That was the way of them. Pan was the boi who didn't cry, but he cried with Wendi when the nightmares came in the night, and now, when everything was falling apart.

16

Through the Window

an had to tell the Pirate crew that Hook was gone. Most of them had gone to bed, the party and battles long over. Pan sent me to the upper floor of the Jolly Roger and into the Pirates' barracks to wake them. I shook Smee awake, and he immediately knew from the look on my face that something was wrong. I told him that everyone had to come downstairs to the living room. Smee didn't tease, question, or fight, which surprised me, since we usually scrap with each other over everything; he just looked scared when he got out of bed wearing only a pair of flannel pyjama pants. I'd never seen his chest scars before. He woke the rest of the Pirates, and I led the way downstairs. Everything felt wrong. This wasn't my house to be traipsing through in muddy boots, but Pan told me to do it in a way that didn't allow for questions. I knew that I had to obey.

We all gathered in the living room. Pan stared out the window, his back to the door as we filed in. Wendi stood next to him, her hand on Pan's shoulder. At first glance, it looked like she was comforting him, but then I saw the way her hand shook. All the Pirates and us lost bois were seated, on couches and carpet, in the very room where last night I'd swung from the ceiling under Hook's hands. Pan isn't one for fancy words. I could tell by the way he cracked his knuckles that he was upset. Wendi had taken a seat on the arm of the couch.

"I don't know how to tell you this ..." Pan began, his voice cracking and trailing off. He cleared his throat and continued. "The Crocodile won, but it can no longer chase him. Hook is gone."

I couldn't imagine what any of the Pirates were thinking or how they were able to process this news, but they acted properly as Hook's men, even now, holding strong and stoic. He had trained them well. He would have been so proud of their good form.

There wasn't anything else for Pan to say. We didn't go back to Neverland right away but caught a couple hours of sleep in the living room when the Pirates returned to their barracks. I don't think any of us slept very well, but I must have dozed off for a while, because when I woke the bois were asleep. I had to blink hard, confused at what I saw. In the darkened room, in the very chair where earlier Hook had sat watching me, now sat Pan. It was like seeing a ghost. Wendi was curled on the carpet at his feet. Pan's green hoodie lay over her like a blanket.

Pan hadn't been able to sleep at all, and when he saw that I was awake, motioned me to follow him downstairs into the dungeon and Hook's study. Pan handled the paramedics and police, who of course had to be called. He ordered me to clean the dungeon. I removed the condoms, cocks, and ropes, stashing them in treasure chests that were decoratively scattered around the play space. Everything looked normal by the time the police knocked at the door. As I cleaned the dungeon, Pan alone took care of Hook—that wasn't something he made any of the grieving Pirates do. Pan knew that Hook would have done the same to protect his lost bois, had their fates been reversed. I answered the door for the paramedics, but it was Pan who had to answer all the questions from the cops about what had happened, but really, there weren't many. The empty syringe lay on the desk where Hook sat slumped, and the cops don't care much about junkies. They just wanted to get out of the house. Before they took him away, Pan kissed Hook one last time, but for the first time tenderly, on the forehead. When the paramedics left, Pan locked the door and went back downstairs. Hook's leather jacket still hung on the back of his chair. Pan ran his fingers along its hard, smooth seams before picking it up and slipping it onto his shoulders.

Wendi had woken when the police left and followed Pan and me down the stairs. He saw her enter the study as he pulled on Hook's jacket. She looked upset but said nothing, and he held her stare silently.

The next few days seemed to work in slow motion. It was

horrible to climb into my hammock each night. I wanted to just quickly pull the bandage off and leave. I was surprised that Pan let us stay, but he was in shock, momentarily weakened. He let Mommy take charge, even though she didn't put her apron back on, and he never commented about the missing stone on her ring. Mommy said that we couldn't just leave Pan, that running away from someone who was hurting wasn't what her good bois should do. She told us that he needed us, and I think she hoped that, now that Pan had lost Hook, he would come with us.

Wendi also spent more time with John Michael. Neither of them had seen death before. They didn't mention Hook at all; instead, they talked endlessly about Mr and Mrs Darling, about how well the Darlings had treated them, how much better than all the other group homes they had been in. They discussed how pleased the Darlings would be with all of us. Wendi also busied herself caring for the Pirates, who joined us for meals now, here in Neverland. It was peculiar to have our battle partners sitting down to packaged noodles with us, but they were without a Captain. They did not speak of Hook either, but always proudly wore his uniform and didn't stay past dinner. Pan never talked about Hook, but that's the way with him. I think if he remembered, the pain would've been too much. It would've destroyed him.

In those final days, Pan talked mostly of mothers, not Mommies, about the distinction between the kink and the biological kinds. Pan hated mothers, always had, and his

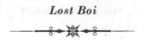
temper seemed so much closer to the surface now. He would never have admitted it, but I think he hoped not only that we might stay, but that he would break protocol and allow us to. In part, I wanted to give that to him and believed that I truly owed him that, after everything we'd been through together.

In the evenings, when the Pirates had returned to the Jolly Roger and when John Michael was with Wendi in the kitchen talking about the Darlings' home, speaking in whispers about the classes they would take, the conferences they might attend, and the lives that awaited us, Pan and I would sit together. He knew that we were leaving, but we never talked about my broken promises, the leaving, or my flight with Hook. He was unusually kind to give me that.

I wish I could say that Pan and I talked about important things: Leather, the life we had together, or even death. Instead, we fucked because it was easier than talking. When we did talk it was about stupid shit, about dramas at the Lagoon, what the pigeons were thinking about, and our favourite candy. I wanted to talk about real things, serious things—I wondered what he thought of the decision I had made and if he would ever forgive me—but we didn't. He monologued about the evils of mothers: the way that they mistreat their children, how they go away, how, above all, they shouldn't be trusted. I completely agreed with him. I hated mothers, and I didn't want to be with Mrs Darling in her home. I didn't want a mother, I wanted my Mommy Wendi. I wanted a life with her, the life that we had promised to one another and were going to build. I saw Mrs Darling as an unpleasant side effect that I could do my best to ignore. Pan wanted me to remember that mothers are evil, that they constrain, control, and abandon. He wanted to ensure that I knew what I was leaving him for, and that it would not be just the magical life that I imagined.

The week after Hook drowned, it was time for us to go. I don't know how that was decided. It was between Pan and Wendi, and neither of them told me. I awoke in my hammock, and Wendi was in the kitchen, making coffee as usual. She told me that I had to help her to get all the bois packed, that tonight we would be leaving, going back through the window to her world. I wasn't ready, but I said, "Yes, Mommy." I packed my bag that day and helped the other bois to do the same.

I snuck out around lunchtime, just me with Washington perched on my shoulder. We made our way to the Lagoon. I hadn't seen Siren since the night that Hook died, since the night I told her I was leaving and she'd slapped me. I wanted to see her one last time, to explain that although I was leaving Pan's world, I didn't have to leave her. I stood on the sinking front steps of the Lagoon and knocked and knocked on the red front door until my knuckles bled, and still they wouldn't open for me. Siren would not grant me access, would not agree to see me. I guess I couldn't blame her.

I walked back to Neverland alone. When I got there, I was surprised that Pan wasn't there. Wendi didn't know where

he'd gone, and she acted nervous as she packed her bags. Pan had agreed to help us get to the Darlings' home that evening, and Wendi feared he wouldn't keep his word and she would have to find the way herself, which she didn't know how to do. I knew he would be back, that he would keep his word and come for us.

Pan left Neverland not long after I went to the Lagoon. It wasn't until much later that Wendi and I learned that he'd retraced, in reverse, the route that he'd first taken with Wendi and John Michael and found himself at London Street, at the door of the Darlings' Home for Girls. Pan picked up the brass door knocker in his dirty hands. I'm guessing he hadn't known what to do until he was there, and then he did something that was neither strong nor brave nor in good form.

Mrs Darling let him in, against her better judgment, probably only because he seemed like the kind of—boy? girl?—who might know what had happened to Wendi and John Michael. Mrs Darling offered him coffee, and Pan, with unexpected cruelty, told Mrs Darling that her girls had become addicts, that Wendi had flown, that she was meaning to bring back a pack of bois so damaged there would be no saving them. He wanted to scare Mrs Darling so that she would close the window—so that Wendi would have to come back to Neverland. When he was done speaking, Mrs Darling suggested that perhaps it was time he leave. She believed nothing this old butch had told her. All she wanted was her Wendi home, she told Pan, and no matter what kind of entourage she brought with her, the window was open.

Mrs Darling also knew that the law would allow them to continue to collect cheques until the girls turned twenty-one, as long as they were enrolled in school. All summer long, Mr and Mrs Darling had dodged visits from case managers to whom they said that the duo were out visiting friends, at camp, working part-time jobs, but she knew they couldn't keep lying. Eventually, it would be discovered that she didn't have the children. Mrs Darling had no intention of closing the window, for so many reasons.

Meanwhile, all afternoon, Wendi was nervous that Pan wouldn't return before we left, and that she wouldn't get one more chance to see him, to make one more attempt to "save" him. I tried to tell her that Pan had been saved long ago by Hook and pigeons and Neverland and all us bois. Pan had saved himself and would never be the kind of boifriend that she wanted. He didn't want to be saved by Wendi. But I told Mommy that I would do my best to fill the gaps that Pan had left in her heart, that I would try to be the boi/boifriend she'd always wanted. Wendi smiled and pulled me into a kiss, hard and fast. She smelled so good, like antibacterial soap mixed with thrift store.

Pan returned to Neverland just in time to take us to the Darlings, but not before he removed our cuffs. They were locked in place with padlocks, but as we'd sworn ourselves forever to him, he hadn't kept the keys. He put his knife next to our skin for the last time and cut the cuffs from us, severing our relationship forever. What we had been to him and to each other couldn't be contained in that little strip of leather, and yet my hand shook so hard that Pan had to hold my arm steady so he wouldn't cut me.

As we walked to London Street, Tink flew ahead. None of the other pigeons followed. I hadn't known how to say goodbye to Washington. I was naïve then; I didn't think it was a goodbye that needed to be said because we would still see each other in city parks and on sidewalks. I thought I might even keep a bird feeder in the backyard. I didn't know that we would stop talking. I didn't know that I would lose the magic that binds bois like us to pigeons, to wild animals. I didn't know that growing up meant that the magic would die.

It was a quiet walk, follow-the-leader style: Pan first, then Wendi, followed closely by me, then John Michael, and then the other lost bois trailing behind. We all pulled at the collars of our shirts. Wendi had managed to get us polos and button-downs from the thrift shop. She'd helped us tuck them into our jeans, and we stood at attention by the door of Neverland before we left. She looked each of us over, asking if we were sure we were ready to meet the Darlings, making sure that we were ready for our new life and that we looked like it too.

When we reached the Darlings' Home for Girls, Pan kept his distance, hidden in the shadows, camouflaged by Hook's dark leather jacket. Wendi held the knocker in her hand, pausing for so long I thought she might set it down silently against the door and run back into Pan's arms. Or that I might. I took a small step toward Pan, but he did not soften. Looking directly into my eyes, Pan swore: "I said nothing to you about forever. I promised you adventure."

Wendi brought the brass to wood. The door flung open, and we were met with bright yellow light from the hallway. Mrs Darling didn't look at all surprised to see us, but Wendi didn't notice. She was too busy nestling into the Darlings' embrace and then proudly introducing us. I got caught up in the commotion, making sure that the Twins were paying attention. When I looked around, Pan had turned away and was walking swiftly down the sidewalk, away from us, my leather cuff dangling from his back left pocket. Mrs Darling had just been saying that, of course they would take us in, help us get settled in life, that she could be like a mother to us. It was at that very moment that I started to cry, and she thought I was crying tears of relief and gratitude for her words. Stupid. I've never cried over a mother. It was Pan I cried for when I thought I would never see him again and the unbearable weight of my decision settled onto me.

We Grew Up

We'd arrived at dinnertime. Wendi had me help her set the table. She kissed me by the fireplace in the dining room while Mrs Darling was busy teaching all the bois how to mash potatoes and fix green salad. Wendi said we needed to keep "us" a secret for now, that the Darlings wouldn't like us "living in sin" within their proper home. I groaned. These were the parts of the grownup world I had forgotten and wasn't prepared for. Wendi kissed me again, her fingernails tenderly tracing my jaw before pinching my neck. She would make all this worth it. We heard a glass break in the kitchen, the slippery hand of a boi, no doubt. I giggled, and Wendi glared. This was new turf and I had to learn the rules. She pointed at the stack of plates we had left at the edge of the table. The dining room table had a leaf so it could be made long enough to fit us all. Carefully, I put one before each chair. They all matched and none of them were chipped. We were fed dinner—fried chicken and potatoes not from a box.

Mrs Darling made us all shower before bed, even though we insisted we had done so earlier in the day. Foldout beds and air mattresses had been brought into the children's room for us. We were all far too big for this, and it was not the sort of age play I get off on. Mrs Darling tucked us in and stayed awkwardly sitting in the room as we drifted off to sleep on clean sheets. I dozed then awoke startled, not knowing where I was or to whom I belonged.

Mrs Darling was at the window, speaking in whispers to a shadow. As my eyes grew accustomed to the dark room, I realized it was no shadow but Pan, seated upon the old tree, the same one from which he had spied on Wendi. My air mattress was right next to Wendi's bed; thankfully, she had made sure of that. I shook her awake, and before she could protest being awoken from peaceful sleep, she saw Pan at the window and rushed from the bed.

Sitting on the window ledge, Wendi held Pan's hand tightly, as though she didn't fully believe he wasn't just a dream that could slip away. Mrs Darling ignored the display of affection and turned her attention back to Pan, who seemed somehow to have charmed the older woman. Her voice was tender when she said, "It's clear that we both love Wendi."

She spoke gently to him as she continued, explaining that he could have a different life; that he could come in from the cold, eat dinner, take a shower. She said, in exchange for bringing her Wendi home, that she would help him, give him a new start.

Pan looked, for a moment, as though he might change his mind. I'm not sure if he knew I was watching or not.

"Will I grow up?" he asked quietly into the darkened bedroom.

"Of course, everyone must," Mrs Darling replied sweetly.

Pan shook his head, a smirk crossing his face. "Not everyone, not me, not ever."

It was Wendi who spoke next. Of course, this had all been her idea, and yet she somehow hadn't anticipated it would go this way. "But Pan," she whispered, "will I see you again? You'll need someone to do the spring cleaning, won't you? I know how dirty Neverland can get…" Her hopeful voice trailed off.

Mrs Darling sat silently. She seemed to accept that there would be a bargain and that this strange person in the tree outside her window had some hold on Wendi. Despite the ugly things he'd said over coffee just that afternoon, he seemed to care for her Wendi, and had returned her not too much the worse for wear. Mrs Darling nodded her approval, though I don't know if Pan even noticed that; he wouldn't have cared. In fact, he might have told Wendi "no," just to spite this grownup. Pan's eyes looked past Wendi into the bedroom, to the neatly tucked lumps of bois sleeping in beds. Then his eyes came to rest upon Wendi's sweet, white wooden dresser on which lay, neatly folded, the mint-green lace apron he had once tied around her waist. He closed his eyes and for a moment images of his Mommy cooking dinners and cleaning his wounds danced through his memory. Pan opened his eyes.

"I will come for you every year. Neverland will await your cleaning, and so will I. Don't forget to pack your apron."

He squeezed her hand as that brave smirk crossed his face. With that, he was gone down the tree and into the night with Erebos, who had patiently waited, lying in the grass. Wendi got back into bed and not long after, I heard the window close, the floorboards creak, and the door squeak as Mrs Darling left our room.

I didn't sleep. I tried counting railroad ties and streetlights that could lead me back to Neverland, but I knew there was no going back. When that didn't put me to sleep, I thought about the classes I would take at school. I thought about the family that I could build with Wendi. I thought of the job I would have, with fucked-up kids like I'd been. I knew I couldn't save them, but at least I could keep them from being alone. I tried to sleep, but I couldn't get Pan's last words to me about adventure and forever out of my mind.

In the morning, I didn't tell any of the other bois that Pan had come. It would have been too hard for them, to know he had been so close but hadn't said goodbye. Besides, they were already so immersed in this new world. There was no sense in complicating things. That's the good answer. I was also selfish, and I wanted to keep something of Pan for myself.

Growing up is so easy for bois; it's remarkable we were able to resist it for so long. The pressures are everywhere:

on the internet, in classrooms, in conferences. "Grow up," everyone says, if you are acting foolish, if you don't have a regular job or a long-term date, if you aren't interested in politics and activism, if you haven't read the right books, if you watch the wrong TV shows. It didn't take long for all the magic and wonder to be forgotten as we saved for top surgery, applied to colleges, submitted proposals to teach workshops. I didn't even realize what was happening to us. The grownup world is so busy, bookended by late-night philosophical debates in bars and buzzing alarm clocks to get to work in the morning.

I had forgotten Pan's promise to come for Wendi in a year's time, but she hadn't. At the end of the first year, everything had changed. John Michael was away at college, studying to be a doctor. Slightly had met a grrrl at a conference, married her, and was living in London. One of the Twins was on a break from college and in rehab; the other joined the military and had just made it through boot camp. Curly was in love with a boi he'd met while working as a security guard at the mall.

Wendi and I had a small one-bedroom apartment. She was in school and writing her stories and I was working overnights at the homeless queer youth shelter. Work was almost like Neverland, except with boundaries. I was still Wendi's boi, and she still tucked me in. She had just finished doing so the night Pan came for her. I don't know how he knew where to find our rundown apartment in the middle of the most bland complex, but there he was, sitting on our balcony, as handsome and cocky as ever, peering through the sliding door, waiting for Wendi to notice him.

Mommy spent the weekend with him. I took on extra overnights, working around the clock. It was too hard to be home alone. On my breaks, I sat in the park, eating my sandwich and throwing pieces of bread to the pigeons. I looked for Washington but couldn't find him. The pigeons wouldn't get close. They stayed on the ground, waiting for me to throw crumbs. They didn't know who I was. They didn't care who I was. It had been a long time since I had last spoken to pigeons. I was worried Pan would keep her, that Wendi would realize what she'd given up. I was also scared that I would remember who I had been and chase after them, trying to catch what we once had. But Mommy came home on Sunday, just like she'd said she would. She cooked dinner for us. I helped chop vegetables for salad. I let the silence sit between us and didn't try to fill it. I've done enough poly to know the coming together again can be strange and disorienting. I let her open up. I waited for Mommy to tell me that she had changed her mind about us, that she was leaving.

"It was strange to be back," she finally said, stirring the mashed potatoes. "Neverland looked just as I remembered from when we left, yet I couldn't figure out how to fit in anymore. It's like the magic was gone, and even though I know nothing has changed, but Neverland was covered in a layer of dust, instead of glitter, like how I used to see it."

Mommy kept stirring and talking. "I tried to ask Pan about Hook." I instinctively sucked air through my teeth.

"He seemed confused, like he didn't really know who I was talking about. I know you told me that when people went away or when they died, Pan wasn't able to remember them, but I didn't think it would be like this. I didn't think he could forget someone whose leather he still wears like another skin!"

I didn't know what to say. I knew all of this, and yet couldn't let myself think too much about it, because I knew what it meant about me and how he wouldn't talk to me, even when he sat on our balcony next to the pots of tomatoes and herbs that Wendi and I planted in the early spring. Wendi and I have built a life together, a cute little life, and Pan didn't ask how I was doing. He didn't even say hello.

"Will you go again next year?" I asked, head down, focused on helping to prepare dinner.

"Of course," Wendi replied, wiping her hands on her apron.

That week, one night after work, Wendi told me to meet her at the mall. She bought me a cinnamon roll at the food court and then led us into the jewellery shop. From her purse she pulled a black handkerchief, laid it on the counter, and carefully unwrapped it. She held out Pan's green glass "stone" to the jeweller.

"I would like to have this emerald set into a pendant. That setting right there would look nice, don't you think, Tootles?" Wendi asked, pointing to a necklace in the case.

"Yes, Ma'am," I said quietly as the jeweller held the stone up to the light and began to inspect it.

Wendi said to the jeweller, "This stone is a priceless family heirloom, it's irreplaceable."

I hadn't known she still had Pan's stone when we left Neverland and was surprised she hadn't done this earlier in the first days of growing up, when she cried out for Pan in her sleep. Wendi must have known what I was thinking because she whispered, "I needed to know he would come back for me."

The jeweller looked up from the stone, flushed, and seemed to struggle with his words. "Miss, I hate to break this to you, but this is nothing more than some cheap cut glass. It's not worth setting into a necklace, but if you like emeralds, I have some nice ones over here." He had carelessly set Pan's stone on the glass counter and walked away toward a display case filled with gemstones.

"You are mistaken," said Wendi. "If I say this is an emerald handed down in my family, then that's what it is, and I would like to have it set in *that* setting right there." Wendi tapped the display case counter with her red fingernail before continuing. "Do you understand? If not, I believe another jeweller will be happy to take care of my family heirloom."

The jeweller stammered an apology, and I tried to swallow a laugh. In that moment, Wendi sounded just like Pan, daring anyone to tell her the world was not just as she said it was. The jeweller managed to compose himself. He carefully picked up the stone and began to examine it again. "I'm sorry,

Miss, I must have been mistaken, it's just as you said; it's an emerald, and a very nice one at that. We will be happy to set it for you. It will be ready on Friday. Will you be paying with cash or a credit card?"

I had to work overnight on Friday, so Wendi went alone to the mall to pick up her pendant. She was asleep when I got home on Saturday morning, clutching Pan's emerald at her throat, which hung from a braided silver chain.

Pan didn't come the next year. I was not surprised and secretly a bit relieved. I worried when Wendi was away, and I was jealous too that I couldn't go back, that I couldn't have a Neverland visit with Pan. He stopped coming, and if Wendi was sad about it, she didn't tell me, but she never took off her emerald pendant. Years passed. Wendi graduated from college but couldn't find a job, so she worked at a coffee shop. She stopped looking for other work, and spent more of her time writing poetry. I got promoted to manager of the shelter. We had a lot more time, a lot more money. Wendi and I moved to a bigger apartment, a loft downtown. We were sellouts, Pirates in our own funny queer way. I didn't see us that way, but I knew Pan would. Ultimately, I learned there aren't "good" or "bad" decisions. Sometimes, decisions are just…decisions. All bois grow up. We get jobs, we work in non-profits, we get married or have civil unions. We are artificially inseminated, or write grants to keep our jobs. We go grocery shopping. We build lives out of the choices that we've made. We make the best lives we can.

I worked my way to the top at the shelter. Now I'm the boss, the manager who gets woken in the night when something has gone wrong. But I still know how to break up a fight, to talk a kid down, to call 911 when someone is overdosing. I never knew how hard it would be. I left Pan to save youth in a different way, to work within systems, to create infrastructure and understanding, to rewrite failed policies. I wanted to do something bigger than Neverland, to give more youth more choices. Maybe Pan had the right idea after all. He's been saving kids every day for decades, giving them home, family, and purpose. I know how much that can mean to someone, how it can be the difference between life and death, how it was for me.

What am I really doing now? Sitting in an office. Making mandated reporter calls to child protective services every time a baby queer kid runs away from some grownups who the law says owns them. I'm turning these kids over to the most evil grownups because some bureaucrat in a suit thinks that's what's best for them, because some researcher who goes "home" every Thanksgiving decided that kids who don't reunify with their biological families are doomed to be depressed or drug-addicted or suicidal.

I like to think that I'm better than those adults I ran away from all those years ago in NYC, but that might just be a story I tell myself. "Actions speak louder than promises," Pan always said. I don't talk about myself at work anymore. When I first started, I talked about who I'd been. When I first started, the kids loved me, and I felt like everything was worth it, like I was making Pan proud, even if he would never know what I was doing. The people I work with don't always see it that way. Once, I accidentally saw a letter from my boss to some board members. She said all kinds of stuff about what a good worker I was, how in any crisis, I was the one that they wanted to call in. But then, the letter went on, she said they needed to be careful how high they promoted me; after all, I would always be a "street kid." My eyes burned. I crumpled the memo and threw it into the trash. Fuck recycling.

I hid in the bathroom for a while, running my fingers along the faded star scars on my right shoulder. When I got home that night, Wendi knew that I wasn't okay. That night, in our bed of fresh sheets, she held me and I cried. No matter what I did, no matter how hard I worked, I would never be good enough. What if everything, every sacrifice, had been a mistake? I cried harder when I remembered the way that Wendi would hold Pan, the same way that she now held me. It was right about then that we started going to play parties and conferences. It was Wendi's idea. She was so busy with budgets and orders at her job running the coffee shop, but she knew that the magic was fading and we needed to do something.

I saw him first. I was at the coffee shop one night, helping Wendi to close up. The month before, we'd bought it from the old owner, and every night, when I got off work, I'd go to the shop and help Wendi: mopping floors, painting walls, hanging art, being her good boi, doing whatever she needed. Jane was there, too. She's a good grrrl. When I got promoted, Wendi and I started spending more time at those Leather conferences, going out and trying to find community, trying to find more folks like us. We met Jane at one of those conferences and were smitten. Little pink pigtails and thrifted dresses, Jane reminds me so much of Wendi when we first met, so perverted and innocent all at once. I found Jane walking around the play space wearing a white dress and carrying a teddy bear cradled in her arms.

I've grown so much since we left Neverland. The world has aged me in so many ways, and I can't always find the magic to be the little boi that Wendi first loved and brought home. We're lucky that we've grown together in so many aspects, but I knew that Wendi missed that little magic. When I met Jane, I saw she was all magic. I felt lecherous, a little like Pan, when I first took her. Of course, she was no baby dyke; she was twenty-one and knew what she wanted, but she hadn't grown up (yet). She still held all the magic, and I knew Wendi would love to Mommy the hell out of that little grrrl. I was right. It was a fast courtship into making Jane our good grrrl. Part of why we got the bigger apartment was to have room for her to move in, and now she works with Wendi in the coffee shop, taking orders and wiping counters.

So, I saw him first. There was so much grey in his red hair, but somehow it only made him look more charming. Pan chose a small table in the front, tossing his backpack onto

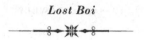
the empty chair before going to the counter. I kept my head turned so he couldn't catch my face. Jane was on register. Pan began emptying his pockets, smoothing out a crumpled bill, and stacking coins. He ordered a coffee with extra sugar and told Jane what a pretty little grrrl she was. Jane blushed; his charms were just as powerful as ever. The shop was quiet, with most customers busy on their laptops or in conversation. Jane took two of the day-old bagels from the container behind the counter and brought them to Pan with his coffee. We keep them there for the street kids who can't get a bed at my work, the ones who spend all night in the coffee shop. Wendi can't bear to see a baby queer go hungry and neither can I.

Pan nodded to the chair across from his and shrugged Hook's jacket onto the back of his chair. It wasn't worn in the way I might have expected it would be, but scuff-free and as clean as on that horrible night when he first put it on. All I could think was that he must have a boi good with leathers back at Neverland. Jane hesitated, looking up at me. Good grrrl, she's such a good grrrl. I nodded my consent. I wasn't sure how Wendi would feel about her sitting there with Pan, falling under his charm, but how could I say no? After all these years, if he had nodded to me, I would have sat in that little chair across from him. Fuck, I would have sat at his god-damn feet if he would permit it. But this isn't about me now, it's about Jane. Pan was talking big, his hands flying in wild gestures. I knew he was talking about Neverland, though I could only pick up stray words—"bois," "pigeons," "battle."

All afternoon, I'd been training new staff at the shelter, who see it as just a job. Some of them are afraid of the youth and seem personally offended when they act like the fucked-up kids they are, when they don't trust us, when they push against boundaries. This isn't where these grownups come from. They don't get these kids, they never were these kids, and they don't understand why I care so much. Sometimes I just want to walk out the door and never come back. Right before I left the shelter for the night, I had to turn two sweet baby street punks away because we were already over capacity, with a wait list stretching into next month for an emergency bed. They didn't even seem surprised. They're used to getting fucked over, used to adults like me not coming through for anything. Sometimes I just want to bring all these kids home with me, but that would make me no different than Pan. I was snapped out of my memory then by Pan's laughter. He looked so much less tired than I felt.

The bell on the door jingled, and Wendi walked into the shop. Her hair was up in a messy bun, but her lipstick was fresh. She carried a big stack of evening newspapers. Without thinking, I moved from my hiding spot in the back to help her. Pan's eyes met Wendi's, then travelled to her neck and the stone that rested in the hollow of her throat. He wasn't surprised to see her. When we bought the shop, she'd changed its name to "Second Star," a reference to Pan's "second streetlight" directions to Neverland. Wendi wanted to be followed by Pan, always. I knew it wouldn't take long. Pan's relationship to Wendi is unique. He's never forgotten her, the way he has forgotten everyone else. Wendi set down the newspapers and ran her fingers through the tendrils that had fallen loose from her bun. Pan's attention had already returned to Jane, this little grrrl that looked so much like his Wendi had the day he first climbed into her window at the Darlings'. Jane had taken a tiny notebook from her pocket and looked as though she was about to read him one of her poems, but stopped and looked to Wendi. I could see Wendi's eyes fill with tears, but she only nodded to our grrrl. We watched them talk and Jane read, and I held Wendi.

It was late when Pan stood to go, pulling on Hook's leather. I heard Jane ask, "Will I see you again?"

A huge smile spread across Pan's face as he nodded, holding her soft hand and closing his tattooed, scarred fingers around it. Pan turned toward the counter where I now stood next to Wendi, but he didn't recognize me anymore. Everything we were, everything we had, everything we shared was gone. Pan's eyes were not sad but distant, as though he didn't quite remember who I was. Wendi walked toward them and pulled Jane in for a tight hug. Then she pulled Jane's chin up so that Jane was eye-to-eye with her Mommy and whispered loud enough for Pan to hear, "My dear grrrl, I will always keep the window open for you."

Jane smiled and walked out the door with Pan into the night, toward Neverland.

Acknowledgments

First and foremost, thank you to J.M. Barrie who wrote the original *Peter Pan*, which inspired this book. Queering his work has been a tremendous honour and a great deal of fun. Thank you to the Lambda Literary Foundation whose ongoing support has been invaluable, and to my beta readers: Fureigh, Kestryl Lowrey, and Sophia Lanza-Weil, who read early drafts of the novel and whose insights were critical to its development, and to my copyeditor Gabrielle Harbowy.

Thank you to Linda Hummer for helping me to believe I had stories to be told. I wish you were here to see this book. Thank you to Auntie Kate Bornstein for dragging me onto the stage and for teaching me to harness the power of anger in my writing. Thank you to the MTA for your endless subway delays, which afforded me the time I needed to write this book. Gratitude to my fellow New Yorkers who offered me their seats after watching me precariously type while standing, and to the iPad I used to write the majority of this book. Also thanks to the bubble tea shop on St. Marks Place in the East Village, where the novel was edited on lunch breaks from my day job.

A very special thanks to Tom Cho, Amber Dawn, and Bear Bergman who introduced me to the amazing folks at Arsenal Pulp Press. A huge thank you to Brian Lam for believing in this story and the entire Arsenal Pulp team, especially Susan Safyan for your insightful editorial feedback and love of pigeons. Working with all of you has been a dream come true.

Tremendous gratitude to Bluestockings bookstore and Bureau of General Services—Queer Division. Thanks to Charis Books and all the other independent queer/feminist bookstores across the United States and Europe that have welcomed me and always carried my books. Thank you to the pigeons of NYC's Washington Square Park who let me study them as I wrote, and the park's human inhabitants who taught me how to befriend them.

Finally, a huge thank you to my Queer and Leather family for believing in me and my work: my dyke moms, my big brother Matthew, and my uncle Toni Amato who always encouraged me to edge play with my writing and create the most dangerous stories I could imagine. This book was made possible by my (not so) tiny menagerie of dogs (Mercury & Charlotte) and cats (Sierra, Noirchat, & Thing) with whom I make a home, and last and certainly not least, for Kestryl, my partner in life and art. Thank you, Daddy, for cooking me

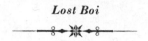
dinner, baking me cupcakes, and taking me to Disneyland. Thank you for beta reading and copyediting, and above all, thank you for building a home that is a magical sanctuary from the grownup world.

Sassafras Lowrey

is a straight-edge·queer punk who grew up to
become the 2013 winner of the Lambda Literary
Emerging Writer Award. Hir books *Kicked Out*,
Roving Pack, and *Leather Ever After* have been
honoured by organizations ranging from the National
Leather Association to the American Library
Association. Sassafras Lowrey lives and writes in
Portland, Oregon, with hir partner and a number
of furry beasts.